Turing Test

Also by the author:

Human Test

Meghan's Dragon

Date Night on Union Station

Alien Night on Union Station

High Priest on Union Station

Spy Night on Union Station

Carnival on Union Station

Wanderers on Union Station

Vacation on Union Station

Guest Night on Union Station

Word Night on Union Station

Party Night on Union Station

Review Night on Union Station

Family Night on Union Station

Book Night on Union Station

LARP Night on Union Station

Career Night on Union Station

Book One of the AI Diaries

Turing Test

Foner Books

ISBN 978-1-948691-14-7

Copyright 2018 by E. M. Foner

Northampton, Massachusetts

One

"That's it for today," I told the secretary. "I'm running late and I can't babysit this thing. By tomorrow afternoon this time—Thursday at the latest—Windows should finish its update."

"Will my laptop finally recognize its power adapter?" Amy asked.

"I can't offer any guarantees. If your boss wants to save money, he should just buy you a new computer every time Microsoft releases a major upgrade. It would be cheaper than paying me to come out every time."

"But then I wouldn't get to see you, Mark. Unless you want to, you know, just meet somewhere? For a drink?"

Uh-oh. I'd been on Earth long enough to know a come-on when I heard one, and getting overly intimate with the natives has been the downfall of many an Observer. I immediately deployed my first line of defence.

"Sounds like fun, Amy, as long as you don't mind my bringing homework along. I'm cramming for the exam, you know."

"Another computer certification?"

"No, I'm taking the 'enrolled agent' test for the IRS," I declared proudly, if untruthfully. "I've been moonlighting as a paid preparer for the last three tax seasons and I'm ready to take the next step. I just wish the federal government was hiring because I'd drop everything to become a real IRS agent."

"You would?"

"I just love taxes, I can talk about them for hours. Have you ever heard of the sixty-five-day rule?"

"No," she said, looking around the office for an excuse to break off the conversation, but most of the other employees had bolted within seconds of the clock striking five.

"You see, trusts have compressed tax brackets, and the trustees may have the option to distribute income—"

"Mrs. White," Amy practically shouted, charging off in the direction of the startled office manager. "I'll get the door for you."

I finished gathering my tools, which consisted of a USB dongle, a multi-bit screwdriver, and my phone, all of which fit into my pockets. My business pays for an unlimited data package so I can use my phone as a hotspot while troubleshooting connectivity problems in small offices. The truth is, it would be easier for me to handle all that stuff over my internal infrastructure, but people on this planet look at you funny if you access their Internet without using any devices.

My last task onsite was to carefully adjust the ancient sheet of carbon paper in my retro invoice pad and make out a bill in duplicate, the top copy of which I left on the secretary's desk. I'd be e-mailing an invoice as well, but I've found that making a paper record on the spot increases the odds of getting paid quickly. And to be honest, I just love using carbon paper. In my three years on Earth I have yet to see anything that comes close to it for elegant functionality or entertainment value.

My trusty Dodge minivan with its inventory of cables and swap-'til-you-drop parts awaited me in the parking lot. I unlocked it from ten steps away and slipped in

2

behind the steering wheel. Another day at the cover-job complete.

The phone in my pocket began to vibrate just as the minivan's onboard system came alive and routed the call through the speakers.

"If It Breaks Service. Mark speaking."

"It's me," a girl's voice announced.

"Hey, eBeth. Is something wrong?"

"You're out of Milk Bones."

"There's another box in the pantry," I told her. "Don't—" but she hung up before I could complete the thought.

Despite her diminutive size, eBeth wasn't one for small talk, which is one of the reasons we get along so well. Most of my neighbors who need a favor feel they have to begin with a story about their hospitalized grandmother and work their way gradually into explaining how I would be saving countless lives if I could get their pirate satellite TV box working again. eBeth always says exactly what she means and lets the chips fall where they may. She's also the only person in the building who Spot didn't hate on sight.

Spot is my adopted canine, or maybe I'm his adopted off-worlder—it's all a matter of perspective. The other day after retrieving his ball from under the couch, it occurred to me that the same is true for everything about our relationship. From my standpoint, it looks like I'm training him to present a paw on demand, to retrieve thrown objects, and to growl at people who want to waste my time. From Spot's perspective, he's taught me to give him treats whenever he offers a handshake, to extract his toys from tight places, and to keep walking when he doesn't like the way somebody smells.

Technically, I'm not supposed to have a dog living with me, but in addition to adding color to my cover story he's a dead ringer for the Archmage of Eniniac, a being so powerful that he can create false records in any information system regardless of the encryption level. Cross an Archmage and you're likely to find that you have a century's worth of unpaid parking tickets for an orbiting spaceship you never even owned.

But Spot was an Earth dog, not an Archmage, and dogs get lonely and bored when they're left alone in an apartment for longer than they feel like sleeping. Before we ran into each other at the dumpster, Spot must have been a street dog, likely a cross between mutts who hadn't had papers in the family going back twenty generations on each side. If you do the math, that's a lot of mutts, but he was smart enough to know a good thing when I popped into town. Maybe the fact I'm not human is what drew him to me in the first place.

I had a deal with eBeth that in return for dropping by to keep Spot company and taking him out for a walk when he felt the urge, she could use my WiFi and a laptop I rebuilt after taking it in as a trade-up. So I didn't feel bad about going straight from work to my real job at the mall on the state highway, just beyond the town line in a lower property tax jurisdiction.

Mark, I answered, silently this time as the call came over my private channel.

We use our code names even on secure channels? the newbie inquired.

Yes, Helen. Immersing yourself in character is the best way to avoid silly mistakes. Is there a problem?

I'm at the location but it looks abandoned.

It always looks abandoned on Tuesdays. Most of the remaining stores have gone to a five-day schedule, Wednesday through Sunday.

Weird. So I just park anywhere and go in?

Some of the others should have arrived by now, and if you leave your car in an isolated spot you're just begging for somebody to break into it. Don't forget to roll up the windows and lock it.

Why? It's a community car.

It struck me that the newest member of my team had only arrived through the portal a few hours earlier and probably hadn't had the time to get approved for any car-sharing services.

Uh, Helen?

Yes, Mark.

How did you obtain the car you're driving?

I was getting acclimated to the planet and familiarizing myself with the downtown area like you suggested. I walked past a vehicle-sharing facility, so I borrowed one.

Could you describe this facility?

Sure. It was four stories high, with a ramp for an entrance, and I could see from the street that it was full of unused vehicles. I just kept trying the doors until I found one that wasn't locked and had the keys in it. The nice man at the booth waved me through without paying, something about a monthly pass. Will they charge me when I bring it back?

Only with grand theft auto, I told her. *Change of plans. Lock the keys in the car and I'll call my police contact.*

Oh. Sorry if I messed that up. But didn't I see a unique identifying tag on the back of the vehicle when I got in? I'm sure I could access—

No, I cut her off. *The first rule is to always stay in character. Just go in and meet the others, I'll be there soon.*

But I think I just found the right database and it's not even encrypted. The security of computer systems on this world is even worse than you reported. I'll just connect to the cellular network and—

Helen! I interrupted again, adding a stern harmonic to my transmission. *Give me the license plate number and I will take care of the car. You will go inside and wait. Understood?*

Yes, mission commander, she replied sulkily. *Transmitting and out.*

I had to brake hard to avoid a swerving car and I instantly noted that the driver was looking down and texting. Humans use the expression 'Blowing up a phone,' to describe when somebody keeps calling or sending text messages. I prefer my own version, taking advantage of the phone's built-in backdoor and remotely reprogramming the device to substitute the Greek character set for texts. The last I saw of the teenager in my side-view mirror, he was shaking the phone upside down as if that would bring the English back.

When I finally pulled in next to Sue's beat-up Corolla fifteen minutes late for my own meeting, I noted with satisfaction that a tow truck was already there loading the car Helen had inadvertently stolen. When I'd called my police contact, I explained that a friend had seen some kids in hoodies get out of the car and run off. In return, Lieutenant Harper made me promise that the police station would be my first stop in the morning, to deal with what he called, 'A minor problem accessing our files.' The police chief's brother-in-law, Stanley, had the towing contract for the town, and he'd evidently rushed right over to be sure of his prize. But why was my newest team member chatting him up?

"Mark," Helen called, waving wildly to get my attention. She was clearly taking her revenge over my insistence that she get into character as a human.

"Helen," I greeted her, stretching my mouth into an artificial smile. "Why are you waiting in the parking lot?"

"Sue said we wouldn't start cleaning until you got here and I wanted to see what would happen to the car. The man made the whole back of his truck tilt, like a ramp, but instead of driving the car up, he hooked the cables underneath somewhere and winched it up the incline. Then he pulled some levers and the whole thing, car and all, tilted back onto the truck. Look, he's doing something under the trunk of it now."

"He has to secure the vehicle so it doesn't move around. We're running late so let's get inside."

"Whatever," she said, proving that at least she'd come equipped with the proper vocabulary for her role as a college girl. "See you around, Stanley."

The driver shot me a guilty nod and then pretended to be fascinated by something under the back of the car. His wife worked as a police dispatcher and he knew that I saw her at the station on a regular basis.

Helen stayed a half-a-step ahead of me and led the way up the concrete walk between the snow-covered shrubs into the once-grand entrance of the mall. The music playing over the PA system had the strange effect of making the concourse seem even emptier than if it had been silent—something to do with the echoes, I suppose. Foot traffic was higher during the day with elderly mall-walkers escaping the cold, but most of them had night-vision problems so dusk was the cut-off. It was just after the holidays, and even when the stores were open, they got more returns than new business.

"You're late again," Sue observed as I followed Helen into the old Border's Bookstore. The fake hardwood floor was almost completely covered with dozens of colorful rugs that were specially designed for easy cleanup of the various fluids and other substances that leaked out of young humans over the course of a day. I was initially skeptical of my second-in-command's idea to open a daycare facility immediately after arriving on Earth, but I took care of creating the various certifications and licenses required. Her calculation that it would be the most efficient way to study pre-schoolers in their natural environment proved to be astute. The location also gave us an alternative place to hold our weekly meetings, though occasionally we would all be stuck waiting for a tardy parent to come and pick up their child.

"I was on a service call and Windows began updating," I explained as we all moved into our starting positions. "You look exhausted."

Sue grimaced at the code phrase as she always did, but the empty concourse of the mall seemed to flicker. I knew that anybody observing the storefront from the outside would now see the pre-recorded hologram of a cleaning team getting to work, while the irritating whine of a commercial vacuum cleaner would foil any potential eavesdroppers.

"He's right," Helen agreed, observing Sue closely. "Is there a problem with your mass-to-energy converter?"

"First of all, we don't speak about mass-to-energy converters on this world, even when we're among ourselves with active shielding," I told the newbie sternly. "Second, she always looks tired by the end of the workday. It's part of her cover."

"Plus, I really am exhausted," my second-in-command added. "Come and help me take care of little children all day and see how you feel. It's physically and emotionally draining."

"Sorry, my assignment is to observe college students," Helen said hastily. "They told me that I'll be the last addition to the team."

"That's right," I confirmed, making it clear through my intonation that I was addressing the whole group. Communicating over audible frequencies by expelling air from the mouth and shaping it with teeth, tongue, and lips had become second nature with me, and I was proud of having mastered some of the nuances of public speaking. True, I had a transponder in my throat rather than vocal cords,

9

but it was calibrated to produce the same vibrations as would be expected from a typical human my size. "We're getting close to the finish line and a few more months should do it, so it's time to start working on our final reports."

"I finished mine already," Paul said, looking up from the plastic abacus he had already spent three meetings trying to figure out, despite the fact I'd assured him that it was a non-functional children's toy. Whether from conviction or sheer contrariness, he maintained that it was a mechanical calculator for computing sunspot cycles. "Humans aren't going to change in the next few months, or the next few centuries for that matter."

"Thus speaks our cynical automotive mechanic," Sue said.

"I wish I was here to work with cars," Helen put in. "From the little I've seen, they're much more interesting than the humans."

"Fixing automobiles isn't the purpose of Paul's assignment," I reminded her. "His job is to assess how humans relate to their vital technology and how well they understand the machines to which they entrust their lives."

"Which is not at all," Paul grumbled. "I could sell most of them muffler bearings and the only thing they'd argue over is the price."

"How about you, Mark?" Helen asked. "What's your assignment?"

"I'm evaluating how humans use what passes as computer technology on this world."

"And how they relate to artificial intelligence?"

"This room contains the only artificial intelligence on the planet."

"I work in elder care," Justin volunteered, stepping forward and giving the newbie a firm handshake. "Most of the old humans are pretty nice, though they have a lot of trouble with their memory subsystems."

"Stacey von Hoffman, the Third," our cultural expert introduced herself. "People in the art world don't take you seriously unless you sound like you come from old money. Welcome to Earth."

"Thank you," Helen replied politely, though her attention had strayed to the final member of my team, who had busied herself wiping down toys with a cleaning solution of her own making.

"That's Kim," Sue told the newcomer. "She works at the town health department and she's here on Earth to investigate human hygiene."

"Did I miss something?" Kim asked, looking up.

"Now that the introductions are out of the way, you all know what comes next," I said. "Who wants to start us off?"

"Do we really have to?" Sue complained. "Teddy White was sick when his mother dropped him off and I had to hold him all day to keep him from crying."

"We have rules for a reason," I told her. "Let's go around in a circle and everybody take one."

"Rule #1. No adoption of native pets," my second-in-command recited unenthusiastically.

"Rule #2," Paul said. "No revealing our presence to natives or unaffiliated extra-terrestrials."

"Rule #3," Justin continued the chain. "No interfering in native customs, however uncivilized they may be."

"Without the commentary, Justin," I said.

11

"Rule #4," Kim said. "No employing our superior technology and intellect in a way that would risk exposing this mission."

My turn had come, and I added, "Rule #5. No recruiting locals for off-planet work until the close of the review period."

"Rule #6," Stacey said. "No looting of cultural artifacts or violating local laws, unless absolutely necessary."

I turned to the newbie. "Care to bring us home, Helen?"

She puzzled for a moment over the expression, and then added in a firm voice, "Rule #7. No going native."

"Great. Now who has news to share? Kim?"

"I've collated all of the data on bacteria I've gathered from local restaurant kitchens and my conclusion is that the signs in bathrooms instructing employees to wash their hands aren't as effective as you would think."

"That's because humans are functionally illiterate," Paul grunted without looking up. "Let's play cards."

"We play games at team meetings?" Helen asked.

"Poker," Justin told her. "It's our canary in the coal mine."

This time she understood the expression immediately. "An early warning system."

"I saved rule #7 for you because going native is the greatest risk for Observers," I told Helen. "We'll know there's something wrong if any of us start displaying human behavior in our betting patterns."

I think the poker-test is best exemplified by the apocryphal AI who long ago took control of the Permeasean Empire's flagship and told her creators to choose between granting full legal rights to sentient machines and death. Artificial intelligence doesn't need to bluff.

Two

By the time the meeting wrapped up, I was out nearly twenty dollars and beginning to wonder if some of my team members were cheating. Sue agreed to give Helen a place to keep her things until our new team member found student housing, and I headed home to check in on Spot before going to my real job. Alright, I might have already said that commanding the observation mission was my real job, but it doesn't pay much by galactic standards. I earned a good hourly rate at my cover job, but there were plenty of expenses involved in living on Earth. My goal was to come away from this assignment with enough credit banked at Library, the AI homeworld, to cover my information needs for the next few decades.

I could see the data stream flowing out of my apartment before I even opened the door. eBeth was sitting on the couch, and Spot was competing with the laptop for attention. Judging by the look of intense concentration on the girl's face, the dog was losing, but he seemed to enjoy the heat from the cooling fan. I discretely sampled a few packets and saw that she was taking on a skeletal dungeon boss with a friend and had nearly depleted the monster's hit points.

"Bingo," she shouted as the skeleton crumbled, dropping an enchanted sword and a purse with twenty gold pieces. I never understood what a skeleton warrior needed with money, but as eBeth told me, I wasn't gamer material.

She completed the quest with a flurry of keystrokes, and then closed the laptop and scratched Spot behind the ear. "Hey, Mark. Were you late for your meeting?"

You could make an argument that eBeth's knowing about my meetings was a violation of the rules, but if you're going to split hairs, I shouldn't have given her a laptop that's basically window-dressing for the Bereftian computing core I'd substituted for the original mother-board. The core was a centuries-old model, so it didn't exactly count as advanced tech, though I could expect to get an earful if word got out in the wrong circles. To say that its computational capacity exceeded that of all the existing microprocessors in the state put together would be an understatement. The laptop now ran Windows in a virtual machine without ever showing an hourglass.

"New team member looks like she'll fit in nicely," I replied to the girl. "Speaking of which, have you thought about what I said?"

eBeth scowled. "I have plenty of friends. You, Spot, Death Lord...." She paused, holding the middle finger of her left hand between the thumb and forefinger of her right as she ran out of names to count off. "Anyway, the kids at school all hated me."

"Did you even go this month?" I asked. I didn't enjoy playing the heavy, but her mother's parenting skills were limited to whipping up a peanut butter and jelly sandwich on a good day, and there hadn't been many of those in the three years since I moved into the building.

"I learn more by myself. School is a waste of time and all of the teachers insist on calling me Elizabeth."

"Socializing with other members of your species is — "

"Can we go already?" she interrupted. "Spot, go for a ride?"

The dog came off the couch like a rocket, jumped up to grab his leash from the coat rack, and brought it to me in his mouth. Most, if not all of my attempts at providing guidance to eBeth ended in a similar manner, but I thought I'd give it one more try.

"Have you ever met Death Lord in person?" I asked, though I suspected I already knew the answer to that one. He was her partner in Caverns of Corruption: Part Four, the massively-multiplayer online role-playing game she had been immersed in when I came home.

"Every time he tanks for me," she replied, using gamer terminology for a warrior with high levels of constitution and strength who could lead the charge and take serious damage, while spell-casters like herself could stand back and deplete the monster's hit points with ranged attacks. "What?"

"I meant in real life—IRL," I said, to make sure she understood. I knew he was a nice enough kid and not some middle-aged stalker because I'd tracked him down when she'd first started partnering with him, just to be on the safe side. He even lived in town on the good side of the tracks, and he still attended high school.

"Real life is overrated."

"As compared to killing innocent monsters all day?"

eBeth shrugged. "Are we going already?"

Spot growled impatiently despite having a tennis ball in his mouth, so I attached his leash and the three of us headed out to my van. I keyed the remote for the cargo door to slide open and then I let go of the leash. Spot raced ahead and leapt in.

"Can I drive?" eBeth asked.

"You don't have a license, you don't even have a learner's permit, and you're not old enough to be behind the

15

wheel at night." I always felt that it was important to remind her of the rules before I handed over the keys. She went around to the driver side, and when I opened the passenger door, Spot had already wriggled through the space above the center console and claimed my seat.

"Back," I told him. "eBeth's driving."

Spot gave me a look of concern, dropped the tennis ball, and grabbed the shoulder-belt buckle in his mouth and strapped himself in. Smart dog.

"Never mind." I clambered in the cargo door and sat on a toolbox. When eBeth had started pestering me about driving a year ago, I had taken the minivan to Paul's shop and had him install servo motors on the steering rack and a wireless transponder on the antilock brakes. If I'd turned around the backup camera to point out the front, I could have driven the van remotely from the other side of town.

Although I've been on Earth a few years already, I sometimes think I understand less about the economic system than I did before I arrived. Why driving instructors aren't among the highest paid employees on the planet is beyond me. Despite the fact that my body wouldn't be harmed by anything as innocuous as an automobile accident and my mind is backed up at Library, there's just something about being in a car with a teenage driver that triggers a primal fight-or-flight response, even in AI.

It took twenty seconds for the motor to move the driver seat from its normal position up to the very front so that eBeth could reach the pedals. Then she adjusted the rearview mirror, the side mirrors, and we slowly pulled out from the parking spot. I flinched at the blaring horn from the pizza delivery guy she cut off.

"He wasn't there a second ago," eBeth complained.

"No, a second ago he must have been a good thirty feet back at that speed. I was watching, and you didn't check the mirror after adjusting it."

"You can't see my eyes."

"Actually, I can. Look in your rearview."

"So how am I supposed to drive with your big, fat head in the way?"

"Just trying to help," I told her. "Turn left."

"I know how to get there," she said, braking hard to make the corner. "You distracted me."

Spot let out a worried whine.

We drove on in silence for a minute before eBeth said, "This jerk in front of me is all over the road. I'll bet she's texting."

I took a break from watching eBeth's eyes in the rear view mirror, and sure enough, I could see the telltale reflection of a phone in the windshield of the car ahead of us. I used the backdoor access I'd discovered to blow the phone up, Greek style.

"What the—" eBeth shouted as she stood on the brakes and simultaneously laid on the horn in an impressive show of hand-foot coordination. My van stopped a few inches short of the Audi's back bumper.

"Oops," I muttered. "Who stops in the middle of the road because they can't read their texts?"

"I warned you that you're going to cause an accident doing that one day," my unlicensed driver lectured me as she backed up without checking the mirrors. She pulled around the Audi in the right lane, splashing a sheet of freezing water running along the curb onto the sidewalk and drenching a group of high school students. Then she looked over her shoulder at me and asked, "Can I take the highway?"

"Yes, take anything. Just watch where you're going," I begged her.

eBeth cut the wheel hard to make the onramp, and Spot made a noise that sounded like he was going to throw up. I reached around his seat to hit the button for his window, and he squirmed around under the safety belt until he could stick his nose out in the wind. Seconds later, he was one happy dog.

"It's the next one, right?" eBeth asked, all business now that she was driving on the highway. The diversion from local streets would add about two miles to the trip, but it was worth it to go straight for a while.

"Main Street, Exit 14." Knowing I would regret the following statement for the rest of my time on Earth, I added, "I never thought I would say this, but you should be driving faster."

She mashed the gas pedal, getting us from 45 to 75 just in time to reach our exit.

"Sorry," eBeth said, braking again. The steering wheel shook in her hands and the whole front of the minivan vibrated. "What should I do? Do I have a flat?"

"Ease off the brakes a second," I told her, and the vibration vanished. "You must have warped a brake rotor when that Audi stopped in front of us back on Elm. I mean, we must have warped a rotor, it's not your fault. It was getting time to replace them anyway."

"Can I keep driving like this?" she asked. "Oh, it's not so bad braking now that we're going slower."

"We'll stay off the highway on the way home and I'll bring the van to Paul tomorrow," I told her. "Just take it easy until we get to The Portal."

Spot gave a happy bark when we turned into the parking lot of my restaurant and training school, which is

18

where I make the real money. I call it a school, but we weren't certified by any accreditation organizations, and as a fully-functioning restaurant and bar, the profit was mainly in the booze. The owner before me had run an actual culinary school, but I was primarily interested in training bartenders and waitstaff, along with providing an informal program in banquet facility management.

Most nights we had a pretty good crowd of people willing to eat what they called 'practice food' for half the price of what you'd pay elsewhere. And the downtown had been depressed for decades, so our main competition was supplied by the VFW, Knights of Columbus, and three places with neon palm trees on their signs. Tuesday nights we featured Karaoke in the banquet hall, and the Prime Rib Special brought out the older price-conscious citizens.

"Evening, Mark," Chief Harrow said to eBeth as she opened the driver door and hopped out next to his cruiser. "You seem to be shrinking."

"We switched after pulling in just to fool you," the girl retorted. "Actually, Spot drove us here."

I got between them quickly and shook the chief's hand. "Not singing tonight?"

"No. Martha has a bit of a sore throat and I'm not getting up there alone."

"Coward," his wife croaked.

"Next week, then," I told her. She jabbed the chief with her elbow.

"What? Oh, and thank you, Mark. You'll have to let me pay next time."

"I'm holding out for a free pass to the police and firemen's cookout on the Fourth," I replied automatically. My staff had strict instructions not to charge the mayor, the fire chief, the police chief, or Lieutenant Harper, and to be fair, all four of those luminaries insisted on leaving the waitstaff generous tips. I also carried a book of dinner-for-two gift certificates with me at all times, just to grease the municipal wheels, so to speak.

The chief and his wife got into the cruiser and headed home, and I followed eBeth and Spot into the banquet facility, through the side door featuring a sign that read, 'No dogs or unaccompanied minors.'

"I'm with him," I heard eBeth tell the new bouncer, pointing at Spot.

"They warned me about you," he said, ushering the pair in before turning to greet me. "Hi, Boss."

"Settling in alright?"

"Piece of cake. The bartender, uh, Donovan, asked me to tell you to find him as soon as you came in."

"I'll do that. Did they warn you about Julio?"

"The guy who thinks he's Julio Iglesias and won't give up the mic?"

"Yes. If it happens, don't wrestle with him. Mary will turn off the Karaoke machine and call a break. It only takes a few minutes for him to snap out of it."

"I'll remember."

I watched eBeth and Spot disappear through the 'Employees Only' door at the other end of the banquet room and then I headed over to the central bar that served the dining room as well.

"Mark," Donovan cried in relief as soon as he saw me. "I just realized that we're out of Jack Daniels and Bud."

"Didn't Jesse show you how to do the ordering last week?"

"Yeah, I don't know what happened. I must have messed up on the Bud because we're out of bar bottles but we've got six too many kegs. And I thought that there was a whole case of Jack in the storeroom, but the box was full of paperbacks."

"Jesse's. I'm letting her store a few things here temporarily until she's ready to have them sent on." I pulled out my wallet and extracted a hundred-dollar bill. "Take this and buy a couple of 1.75-liter bottles of Jack at the SuperPak before they close. You can funnel them into the pour bottle as needed."

"I thought it was illegal to buy retail for a bar."

"Is it? But you're not buying for the bar, you're buying for yourself and loaning it to us."

"Oh. Sorry about the mistakes. I never realized how much work Jesse did around here before she got that sweet job offer from the Australian resort. Between the waitresses, cooks, and bouncers, we must have provided half the staff for that place."

I gave him a wry smile and headed for the door that eBeth and Spot had taken. It led to stairs down to the basement, which was mainly taken by storage. I could hear eBeth in my office peppering Jesse with questions as I made my way around the mounds of broken chairs and frayed tablecloths. Most of the stuff really should have gone into the dumpster, but through some unknown force of nature, it migrated into the cellar instead.

"And they have how many eyes?" eBeth asked excitedly.

"Just four," Jesse told her. "I think the Medusa hair will be harder to get used to, it sort of looks like the females have a lot of little snakes growing out of their scalps."

"Ew, that's so gross. Let me see the brochure."

"Ladies," I said, alerting them to my presence. "Did you finish the paperwork, Jess?

"Yes. And I haven't left the office since you let me in this afternoon, except to grab a roll of toilet paper. I made sure nobody else was down here before I snuck out to get it."

I snapped my fingers in irritation at myself. I'm always telling my team that it's the little things that trip you up, like not keeping toilet paper in your private bathroom. Fortunately, Jesse and eBeth already knew about me, but a mistake is still a mistake.

"I'll make sure not to run out again in the future," I said, closing the office door behind me and accepting the sheaf of papers from Jesse. I checked quickly to make sure that she had filled out all of the proper blanks and signed wherever necessary. "Is that all you're taking? You won't be able to come back until we announce our presence on Earth and get the real system connected, and that's still a few months off."

"I'm sure," she said, nudging her backpack with her foot. "I can't believe that all those funky drinks you taught me to make are actually going to come in handy. I just have to get the substitutions straight in my head and I should be able to slip right into the job."

"I'm sure you'll love it and the Dinkles are big tippers."

"Can I work the portal?" eBeth asked.

Technically, she shouldn't have known about the existence of the portal in the basement of my restaurant, much less how to browse the carousel. The portal was protected by a Level Twelve security field that could only be disabled by my team members, so there wasn't any risk of unauthorized usage. If somebody exploded a thermonuclear device directly over the building, the portal would still exist in the same place, floating in the air at the center of a giant radioactive crater. The League of Sentient Entities Regulating Space has its issues with acronyms in some languages, but they've been building intra-dimensional portals for over fifty million years.

eBeth grabbed the joystick attached to my office computer and turned to face the wall behind the desk. The building was almost a hundred years old, with a red brick foundation that needed repointing, but when I issued a silent command with my entry code, the solid wall was replaced with an inky black tunnel large enough for a baby elephant to walk through.

"All right, Spot," I said. "I'm trusting you here, so let's not have a repeat of last time."

The dog nodded energetically and settled down on his belly, eyes wide and tongue lolling.

"It's the same resort we sent Karen and Dianna to last month," I informed eBeth. "You'll see—"

"A gold reception desk surrounded by giant potted plants that look like pear trees with silver fruit," she interrupted. "Open it already."

I transmitted the selection code to bring up the carousel with some extra parameters to limit the selection to a hundred options so we wouldn't be there all night. The entrance of the tunnel rippled and then was replaced by a sunny beach of pale blue sand on an emerald green sea. Vacationers from a dozen species lounged under large umbrellas, sipping, lapping or siphoning drinks from glasses festooned with umbrellas that matched the unique patterns of the bigger ones providing shade.

"I get it," Jesse said. "The bartender matches the drink umbrella to the shade umbrella so the waitstaff can deliver the order. Is that where I'm going?"

"No, though the resort where you'll be working is also on a beach," I replied. "I've limited the catalog selection to worlds with Earth-compatible atmospheres so—"

eBeth jiggled the joystick, and several scenes blurred past before locking in on a grassy rolling plain that seemed to stretch on forever. A head that could have belonged to a prairie dog popped out of a burrow and regarded us with a quizzical look. Spot was through the portal in a flash.

"—the dog won't asphyxiate if his instincts get the better of him," I concluded. "Spot! Get back in here. You'll never dig him out of that burrow, and you'd only get indigestion if you did."

We all ducked reflexively as clumps of dirt flew towards the portal, but the filter was smart enough not to pass them through. Plenty of people, using the term in its broadest sense, think that the portal filters are there to prevent poisonous gasses from seeping through, but they wouldn't pass sound waves if that were the case. The main purpose of the smart filters was to minimize invasive insect species and airborne spores, but they also prevent fast-moving projectiles from crossing over, and fortunately the ejection matter from Spot's excavation matched the criteria.

"If he does get indigestion, there's plenty of grass to eat," Jesse observed.

"I'm going to count to three," I threatened in my sternest tone. "One. Two. Thr—"

Spot darted back through the portal and gently took the pieces of the Milk Bone treat that eBeth had just snapped in half.

"When you explained about the interdimensional portal, I never dreamed it would be just like stepping through a door," Jesse said.

"Intra-dimensional," my apprentice portal operator corrected her while bringing up the next selection with the joystick. "Interdimensional would mean between different dimensions, and Mark says that we couldn't survive in any of them. Intra-dimensional means within this dimension, where we fit." She nudged the game controller forward, and displaying reaction times that would make a robot jealous, stopped just as the resort's reception desk flashed into existence. "Got it!"

"We're going to miss you around here, Jess," I told her. "Donovan already screwed up this week's orders."

"Good thing it's only Tuesday," she replied, shouldering her backpack. "Shouldn't I be more nervous about this?"

"It's a great deal for both of us. You'll tend bar at the resort for a year or two, learn useful sayings in a few alien languages, and come home with enough money to buy your own restaurant. As long as you stick it out through your initial contract, I'll get a finder's fee that's equal to what I make out of this place in two months for placing an exotic alien bartender."

"Who's the exotic alien bartender?"

"You," eBeth told her. "I've got your Facebook password, and Mark subscribes to an Australian photo site, so I'll keep your page up-to-date. If anything really important comes in the mail, Mark can contact the resort."

"Thanks again," Jesse said, taking a final look around the basement office. "Well, here goes nothing."

She stepped through the portal and strode up to the reception desk without the slightest sign of hesitation. I congratulated myself again on my instinct for people, closed the portal, and restored the security field.

Three

Living around humans must be rubbing off on me because I was starting to feel a little guilty about using official equipment for my personal business. It's not that there was any expense involved, the conservation of energy just doesn't work that way in portal dimensions, but technically I was violating the terms of my employment. Rather than hanging around for the singing, I brought eBeth and Spot straight home and then spent the night cut-and-pasting from Wikipedia to create a voluminous report on the history of human technology. I'll probably get the "Best Observer" reward at the next banquet.

First thing in the morning, before regular business hours, I brought the minivan by Paul's garage. He was already at work, which wasn't surprising since none of my team benefit from sleep. When I lifted the roll-up garage door, Brutus shot out past me, tail-stump wagging, then stopped in disappointment.

"Sorry, boy," I told him. "Spot's at home sleeping."

Brutus snorted and began to head back inside, then he changed his mind and went on fence patrol, no doubt hoping to scare an early morning jogger. The runners never seemed to figure out that for all of his snarling and jumping at the chain-link fence, the dog always stopped before the driveway, which wasn't even gated. Brutus was on the garage's payroll as a security specialist, if you were wondering. Not a pet at all.

"What's up, mighty leader?" Paul asked, popping out from under an SUV on his home-made mechanic's creeper. It looked just like a regular creeper, but the wheels were only there for show. He'd actually converted it from a hoverboard, a real one, not one of the motorized things humans wheel around on. I never inquired about how he had smuggled it through our portal without triggering the advanced technology alarm but my guess would be some form of Rynxian cloaking technology. At least, that's how I bring in the goodies that help make life on Earth bearable.

"eBeth had to slam on the brakes for some idiot stopped in the middle of the road," I explained, skipping over the part where I had blown up the idiot's phone. "Somebody must have cracked open a fire hydrant nearby, because she drove through a deep puddle going around the car and the cold water didn't mix well with the hot rotor."

"Puddles in the middle of the winter," Paul said, shaking his head. "So why didn't you fix it?"

"Where am I going to find a rotor in the middle of the night?" I responded.

Come on, don't play dumb. You could have taken off the wheel and straightened that rotor between your palms.

If I was an advanced AI inhabiting a very expensive encounter suit rather than a human, you mean. Just treat me like you would any other customer.

"Alright, Mark. Let me just put it up on the lift and we'll see what the problem is." He took the keys from me, drove the minivan into his second bay, then started removing lug nuts with an air ratchet before the lift was done moving. He pulled off the driver side front wheel and made a show of inspecting the damage. "Yeah, warped all right. You're looking at eight hundred bucks for new rotors and pads all around. More if I have to bleed the system and retrain the anti-lock processor bearings."

"What! I just checked online and I can get all four rotors and pads for under $150 with free shipping."

"I know you're kidding, sir, because I don't see a smartphone in your hand. I can show you the invoice from my parts supplier if you want. All I'm charging is the book labor."

"What if you only change the one rotor?"

"My insurance would never allow that. You did say to treat you like any other customer."

I wilted in defeat. "Alright, just fix it."

Paul gave me a wink, whistled for Brutus to stand watch, and lowered the garage door. He added some thick washers to the wheel studs and put the lugs back on to hold the rotor, then started the van and shifted it into drive. We both watched the rotor spinning and it was obviously several mils out.

"Cheap steel," Paul commented, pinching the rotor between his thumb and forefinger until the metal began glowing a dull red. Then he grabbed two heavy steel blocks from his workbench, one in each hand. He crouched a little to get his eyes in the right position, killed the engine remotely and slammed the blocks together on the rotor, one from each side. "Bet you I got it on the first try."

"How much?" I asked, having my doubts about the success of the operation. I'd seen similar chunks of steel lying around every serious welding shop I'd been in on

Earth, but I always assumed they were off-cuts used for doorstops or spacing. Learn something new every day.

"Double or nothing on the repair?"

"And what's getting doubled?"

"Well, there's the facilities I have to pay for, you know. The lift, the air compressor, my labor. How about twenty dollars?"

"Done."

Paul restarted the engine and shifted into drive again. We both watched the rotor spin a few hundred times, then I got out my wallet and handed over forty dollars. He stuck it in his breast pocket.

"How about a receipt?" I asked. "I can take that as a business expense."

"A receipt will cost you a hundred. If you figure my own taxes, insurance, workers comp—"

"Never mind," I interrupted and killed the engine remotely myself. "Other than cheating on your taxes, are you keeping your nose clean?"

"You know me," Paul replied, which was exactly what I was worried about. "What are you doing out so early anyway? I thought you'd be home making your human breakfast."

"She's not my human and she takes care of herself," I shot back, even though I sensed that he was baiting me to change the subject. "We've only got a few months to go before we can tell the whole world we're here, and it would be nice to make it without any incidents. Oh, and I'm out this early because I promised to go fix the booking computer at the police station."

"Tell them to stop watching porn."

"They claim it's part of the job. Anyway, if it's the same ransomware outfit that nailed them last time, I'm going to consider taking a vacation to Russia and paying a visit."

"Now who's causing incidents," Paul said. He spun off the lugs and washers, remounted the wheel, and snugged it home with the air ratchet. He checked the final torque between his thumb and forefinger. "You watch out for those hackers. They take threats to their business model seriously."

"And you know this because?"

"I know lots of stuff," he said, dropping the van faster than OSHA standards should have allowed. Outside, Brutus barked twice. "That's his 'customer' bark. I'll get the door, you hop in and back out of here so I can make some real money."

"See you next Tuesday," I called through the window as I drove past him. On the way downtown I stopped at a drive-through to buy a box of donuts, and three minutes later I pulled into the municipal parking garage where Helen had stolen a car the previous afternoon. It was still three-quarters empty at this hour, and some of the cars were town vehicles that were garaged there when they weren't in use. The impressively titled 'skywalk' which soared fifteen feet over Taft Ave led into Town Hall, the basement of which was shared by the police department and the tax assessor.

"We've been locked out of the system all night," the desk sergeant greeted me. He pointed to the holding cell. "I had to book those clowns on paper."

"In duplicate?" I asked, wondering if the sergeant knew about carbon paper.

"Naw. I couldn't find the old forms so I just got their particulars down." He indicated some napkins from a

Chinese take-out place that were now liberally covered with indecipherable printing and doodling. "I'll enter everything as soon as you fix it."

I placed the box of donuts on the counter and sat down in the rolling office chair at the computer used for booking. The screen showed instructions for paying ransom in Bitcoin in return for a decryption key to recover the hard drive's data. All of my team do a little Bitcoin mining on the side, since we're overpowered for our assignments and the money is just sitting there, but I wasn't about to hand any of mine over to a hacker.

"Any of the other machines affected?" I asked the sergeant. I inserted my custom recovery USB stick in the front-panel slot and rebooted the machine. Rather than containing an image of the hard drive, the device served as a high-speed wireless bridge to one of my built-in networks. When the screen came to life, I bypassed everything and began restoring the system from my internal backup.

I know, you thought I was going to retask one of my quantum computing processors from working on a weather forecast for the weekend to cracking the encryption. Sure, I could go that route if I wanted to, but let me tell you something about AI. Just because we're really good at math doesn't mean we get our jollies factoring for prime numbers or computing pi to a superfluous number of decimal places. There's a reason that scientists and engineers use the term 'significant figures' to describe the digits that actually contribute to results. There's fun math and there's boring math. Cracking the crude encryption humans use falls into the latter category.

"I don't know if any others are affected," the sergeant finally answered after swallowing another mouthful of donut. "That's the only computer they let me on."

"This will take a bit of time and you'll lose any records you entered after 5:00 AM yesterday," I told him, that being the last time I had illicitly made a remote incremental backup of the system. You would think that some of my clients, especially the police and the medical offices, would wonder why I always seemed to have an up-to-date backup of their confidential data. But human nature is funny and they're always too happy to get up and running again to ask questions.

"Great. Are you going to update our whatchamacallit software so it doesn't happen again?"

I pushed back my chair and shook my head. "The best security suite in the world can't help if you guys keep visiting compromised websites and opening attachments."

"I only open attachments from people I know," he protested.

"The return address on e-mail is no different than on regular mail," I said, brandishing an envelope that was lying on the desk. "You can write whatever you want on there and the post office will deliver it."

"Isn't that illegal?"

The young men in the holding cell who had been following our conversation for lack of anything better to do with their time burst out laughing.

"Yeah, you go and arrest everybody who spoofs an e-mail address, Sarge," one of them suggested.

"I saw a story on the Internet that quantum computers are going to break all of the encryption systems in the world," the other prisoner remarked. "That's why I keep all of my money in cash, like I was trying to explain last night when the detective grabbed us."

"Yeah, me too," his companion said. "Since when is it illegal to go around with a few thousand dollars in your pocket?"

"And the drugs?" the sergeant asked tiredly.

"I don't know anything about any drugs. I swear the lab test will come back negative, and if it doesn't, that's because the chemists are all high. I read another story on the Internet where—"

"Shut up and I'll let you have a donut," the sergeant interrupted. Both of the young men stopped talking immediately.

"Morning," Lieutenant Harper said, coming around the counter. "Got everything under control, Mark?"

"It'll take another twenty minutes but you're only going to lose a day's worth of data," I told him.

"And there's no way we can track these guys down and put them in jail?"

"Oh, you could bring in the FBI and eventually they'll tell you that it's some group working out of Russia or North Korea, but what's the point? The real issue is getting your guys to stop surfing the web for—"

"I know, I know," he cut me off. "Grab yourself a coffee and come into my office for a minute. I want to talk to you about something."

I found my personal mug, which should give you an idea of how often I get called to the police station, and filled it from one of the portable urns at the coffee station, choosing the local Roaster's blend that eBeth likes. All of the departments in town hall had outsourced their coffee production to the start-up owned by one of the mayor's nieces, and from what I hear, the coffee is doing more than the mayor to keep the town running smoothly. I followed the lieutenant into his office and took a seat, prepared to nod sympathetically at some lame excuse as to why his own computer had been ransomed.

"There's no easy way to say this, Mark, so I'll come right out with it. Your friend Kim is too good at her job."

"I don't know what you mean," I said, simultaneously accessing the health department's database to check on her performance reports. Had somebody really figured out that she was posing as human based simply on her stellar work? No, there weren't any special notes in her personnel record.

"When you said an old school friend had moved to town and was having trouble finding a job in her field, I was happy to make the recommendation. But she comes in early, stays late, never makes mistakes, and worst of all, she's too strict on inspections. You've got to explain to her how things work around here."

"You mean the other inspectors are complaining?"

"Mark, we only have three inspectors in the entire department and one of them is the manager. Everybody is complaining, and I don't just mean town hall employees. She's too by-the-book. Didn't she even hit you with a fine?"

"I kind of challenged her to find anything wrong," I admitted. "She got us for mold in the ice machine, some minor documentation lapses on locally sourced ingredients, and a dog in the kitchen when I brought Spot to the meeting without thinking about it."

"You've got mold in your ice machine?" the lieutenant asked with obvious concern.

"Not anymore."

"Just talk some sense into her," the lieutenant said. "It's a small town and we all have to live together."

"Will do. Is there anything else?"

"Well, as long as you're here," he said, and spun his monitor around so I could see the familiar ransomware message. "It must have gotten in over our local network or something."

"That sounds probable," I lied. "I'll just grab my miracle fix-it stick from the booking computer as soon as it's finished there."

"Don't forget your coffee," he said as I rose from the chair.

"Right."

I had various ways of disposing of the food and drink I took in for the sake of appearing human, but I hated waste, so I took a long swallow and shunted the coffee into a clean holding unit I could drain for eBeth later. She claimed that it was even better reheated.

Back in the main office, the restore process was around sixty percent complete, so I pretended to be as entranced by the progress bar as your average human and got going again on my weekend forecast for Kansas City. You'd think that predicting the weather for a landlocked place would be easy, but it doesn't work that way, and I've been competing in a contest sponsored by the cable weather channel to see who can offer the most accurate forecasts there over the full winter. We're graded on high, low, and average temperature, precipitation, and severe weather events, like thunderstorms, hail, or tornados.

I'm currently in second place behind some farm kid who actually lives there, which I think is cheating, though he probably doesn't have access to the same military radars and spy satellites I'm tapped into. You can think of it as a battle between man and machine. I crunch the numbers while the kid bases his forecasts on how the animals act and the way the air feels. Thanks to the prize, there are 21,939 people participating in the contest, so being in second place is no small feat.

An hour later, I was done at the police station and had detected a blind spot in the radar grid that could theoretically allow a foreign power to slip in a nuke designed to maximize an EMP burst in the high atmosphere. I wasn't worried about that, but the coverage hole shaved about point two percent off the reliability of my weekend forecast. I figured that filing an anonymous report with the proper military agencies was just begging for trouble, so instead I did a little remote programming during my drive home and fixed it for them.

Four

I was diligently working on a report update when I heard the dog whining and scratching at the front door. It was unlikely that he wanted to go out at two in the morning, so that could only mean one thing. I turned the handle slowly in case eBeth was already asleep with her back to the door, but Spot had picked up on her presence almost immediately.

"You can let yourself in, you know," I told her for the third time in a month. "You have a chip-key."

"I don't want to get you in trouble," she said sleepily. "What would people think about a teenage girl going into your apartment in the middle of the night?"

"If the neighbors see you in the hall sleeping against my door, they'll think I got you in trouble and threw you out," I countered.

"What?" eBeth came wide awake and turned red. "Ew. I meant that I didn't want to get you in trouble if your supervisor suddenly shows up or something. It's not like I can say I was taking care of the dog in the middle of the night."

"I'm not supposed to have a dog," I told her, going to the closet and retrieving a blanket for the couch. "Don't worry about me. Observers all work on the honor system and there's nobody watching us."

"You don't have a boss?"

"I report to my world's current representative on the League's executive council. But an advanced AI isn't going to decant into a fake human body just to come and check up on me. Our mission to evaluate Earth for membership probably seems like a dragged out process to you, but in our terms, the whole thing will be over in a blink of the eye."

Loud laughter came from across the hall and I turned down my audio gain so I wouldn't have to listen to it.

"Why does my mom do that to herself?" eBeth asked angrily, though I could tell she didn't really expect an answer. "He'll just leave in the morning and probably steal something on the way out."

I gave Spot a nudge with my foot and followed it up with a, 'Go over there and make yourself useful,' look. The dog was happy to oblige since it involved two of his favorite things in the world, sleeping on the couch and eBeth. The two of them settled in and I draped the blanket over them. For a creature covered with hair, Spot was strangely sensitive to the cold.

"Thanks, Mark," she said, burying her face in the dog's neck.

I turned off the light and went back into the bedroom, picking up the report update where I'd left off. After tens of millions of years, the Observation Service had developed a series of universal fill-in-the-blank forms for grading the achievements of candidate populations. Observers were given some leeway in determining which forms were relevant to their study, but the bean-counters expected detailed explanations of every decision. In the end, it was almost as tedious as cracking public key encryption systems. The sun seemed to take forever to put in its morning appearance, and I went out to wake eBeth for school.

"I'm not going," she said flatly.

"You can't just drop out of school," I told her. "You might want to go to college when you're older and they won't take you if you haven't graduated high school."

"Actually, they will. I can just take a bunch of tests if I want to go, but what's the point? It's not like the Vrixian Coherence recognizes academic degrees from Earth."

"I never should have told you about the Vrixians. I thought it would inspire you to go to school."

"It did. It inspired me to go to one of their schools."

I gave up. "Eat some breakfast before you take Spot out. And I've got a cup of Roaster's if you want to reheat it."

"Thanks. Just think of all the food you'd waste trying to maintain your cover if you didn't have me and Spot to help." eBeth went into the kitchen and poured the remains of a box of dry cereal into a bowl, sniffing at the milk from the fridge before adding it. Then she micro-waved some scraps I brought home from The Portal, just to take the refrigerator chill off, and put them in the dog's dish. She saved reheating the coffee and slicing a banana over the top of her cereal for last.

"Don't you miss eating?" she asked me after a couple of minutes.

"How can I miss something I've never done?"

"But you have to consume energy," she reasoned. "Does electricity come in flavors?"

"Not exactly. So what are you going to do all day if you don't go to school?"

"I'll come with you. I want to see how you recruit Jason."

"I shouldn't have told you about that either," I said, more to myself than to eBeth. "The other members of my team have started referring to you as my secretary."

"Shouldn't I get paid then?"

I could have pointed out that she was eating my unused groceries and drinking my recycled coffee, but to be fair, I had gotten into the habit of letting her take care of tasks that required a physical presence. I suspected that my team members were all giving her small jobs as well, but I didn't want to know.

"All right, you can come with me this morning and see how it goes with Jason. Maybe having you there will actually help, but I'm driving."

She exchanged a triumphant look with the dog as if they had planned it together, and for all I know, maybe they did. Twenty minutes later, we were stuck on the highway in one of those flash traffic jams, in this case caused by a Christmas tree on the road. I guess the guy thought that gravity would keep it in the bed of his pickup, even with the tailgate down. Either that or he had planned it as a way to get rid of the tree now that the holidays were over. eBeth honked the horn impatiently.

"Never draw attention to yourself when you're doing something illegal," I told her. "I shouldn't have let you drive in rush hour."

"It's part of being your secretary," she retorted. "The steering wheel didn't shake at all when I hit the brakes. Paul did a good job."

"Stop changing the subject. Get the driver's permit questions from their website and I'll pay for the test."

"Really? Don't you have to be seventeen?"

"Sixteen. You'd know all this stuff if you ever went to school. You'll need your mother to sign the form."

"I signed my report cards for years before I stopped going so I guess I can sign this too. Oh, look. The right lane is open now."

"That's the breakdown lane," I told her as she swung to the right and accelerated past the jam. "You can get a ticket for this."

"But our exit is right here. I'm just getting off early."

"eBeth. We have to talk—"

"I'm sorry, I won't do it again," she interrupted, attempting to look contrite at the same time.

"This isn't about your driving. My meeting with Jason is a serious thing for him and you can't interrupt with questions every minute."

"I'll be good," she promised. "What are you going to do if he isn't interested?"

"Offer him a job repointing the foundation. It really needs doing."

"That would be a huge step down from restoring a church, wouldn't it?" eBeth asked as she took the exit ramp and headed for the restaurant.

"That's one of the reasons I'm hoping he'll go for my offer. Jobs like the church don't come up very often because there just aren't that many stone buildings in town and they're well built. And I think it would do him good to have a real change of scenery."

"You mean from his ex-wife."

"That too," I admitted.

Despite the traffic jam we were still ten minutes early, but Jason's beat-up old pickup was already there. He got out with two coffees when we pulled up and gave eBeth an apologetic look. "Sorry, kid. I didn't know you were coming."

"That's okay," she said. "I'll have his leftovers."

41

"Thanks for coming, Jason." I gave his calloused hand a carefully calibrated shake.

You might be surprised, but shaking hands was one of the most difficult challenges I encountered in passing myself off as human. Without that arcane ritual, I could have gone for years at a time without touching anybody on this planet, even accidentally. The first few times I shook hands with people they looked at me funny. One small business owner who had called me for a quote on a point-of-sale computer even told me he couldn't trust a man with such a limp handshake and wished me well. I went to a major trade show in the city a few days later where I had the opportunity to shake hands with so many salesmen that I finally got the hang of it.

We both turned at the series of beeps from the keypad as eBeth unlocked the restaurant's side door.

"Good little helper, isn't she," Jason commented. "Shouldn't she be in school though?"

"You try convincing her," I told him as we followed in eBeth's footsteps. "I invited her to sit in on our meeting this morning, but if it bothers you…"

"No, I'm just surprised you didn't bring the dog."

"He had a long night," I explained, drawing a funny look from the stonemason. "My office is in the basement."

eBeth was already there sitting quietly in the corner when I showed Jason in. He cast a professional eye over the old lime mortar that was turning into sand between the courses of brick.

"They make some new caulk types you could try if you don't want to go the full repointing route," he said, which was either a brilliant negotiating tactic or a gentle way of telling me he wasn't interested.

"That's not why I asked you to come in, Jason."

42

"You said you had a job for me. Something challeng-ing."

I took a bottle from the deep file drawer of my desk and poured a shot. "I know this is going to sound funny, but I want you to drink this for me."

"Tequila? At 7:30 in the morning?"

"I recycled the bottle. This is something to keep you from remembering the conversation."

"I don't know, Mark," Jason said after a moment's hesi-tation. "You're a nice guy and you run a decent place, but..."

"I'll drink one too," eBeth offered.

"Does this have anything to do with all of the staff turnover around here?" Jason asked in a sudden flash of insight.

"That it does," I admitted.

"And it's why you were sounding me out last week on whether I would move for work, even if it meant the other side of the world."

"Like Australia, sort of."

"Oh, what the hell." Jason took the glass and threw back the contents. "If you're planning to chop me up into little pieces and bury me in the corner, I guess you can just pull out a gun and shoot me. It's not like anybody would hear it down here."

"What I'm about to tell you may sound a little unbeliev-able at first, which is why I wanted to have the conversation in my office where I could give you a demon-stration. The drink you just swallowed takes effect almost immediately. It simply prevents you from forming new long-term memories until it wears off in around a half an hour."

"So you're going to tell me stuff and I won't remember two minutes later?" He snorted. "What's the point of talking then?"

"You'll remember long enough to make a decision, and you'll probably be able to recall coming down here, having this conversation, and then it will just be fuzzy. But so far everybody I've asked has taken the offer, so the forgetting part didn't matter."

"What's the pitch?"

"I'm an artificial intelligence construct from another world." I was forced to wait while he dissolved in laughter, and I glared at the girl when she joined in. eBeth just waved a hand in front of her face and failed to regain her composure. "Fine," I continued. "Watch this."

I picked up the empty shot glass he had replaced on the table and crushed it in my hand, increasing the pressure and pouring in heat until it liquefied. After showing the molten lump to my audience, I rolled it out between my palms, did a little quick shaping, and pulled a tail from the back just before it solidified. I blew on the finished product and held it out for their inspection.

"What is it?" eBeth asked.

"A manta ray," I told her, disappointed that it wasn't obvious.

"It would have worked better with darker glass," Jason said, but he was looking at me now rather than the glass fish. "I've seen magicians do some pretty unbelievable things. You might have had the manta ready and switched it when we were distracted."

"I'm not going to peel away my skin to demonstrate I'm not human because it's too much work to restore it without the right equipment. How about I do this?" I activated the portal and brought up a view of the construction site on

44

Hopi Seven. "That's not a picture. It's really just a few steps away."

"And you came all the way to Earth in search of cheap construction labor?" He was trying to sound sarcastic, but I'm pretty sure I had him hooked from the moment I zoomed in on the flying buttresses.

"Technically speaking, the recruitment of skilled labor from your planet isn't part of my job description," I told the stone-mason, omitting to say that it actually went against the rules. "I couldn't help myself in your case, especially when I know how much you would benefit from a change of scenery. I worked some time as a labor agent before I got tapped for my current assignment."

"Which is?"

"Evaluating humanity for membership in the League of Sentient Entities Regulating Space. My mission is to help determine your world's starting level. We're going to be announcing our presence to the world in a few months, but you would be the first human on this job, so you'll be first in line for species foreman when more people get work there."

"And your space empire needs stonemasons?"

"Good stonemasons, of which you are one. I took the liberty of making a series of images over the course of the year while you were doing the restoration work on the church and I sent them all to the cathedral. They're prepared to offer you an initial five year deal for—well, if you converted the value into gold at the current exchange rates and brought it back to Earth, it would come to over two hundred thousand a year."

"Dollars?" His voice hit a higher note than one might have expected from a barrel-chested man.

"Yes. There are no payroll taxes where you'll be going, and your employer provides all the necessities for living onsite. I have to warn you, though, that until they get more humans, the food will be rather bland."

"What difference does the number of us make?"

"It's easy enough to synthesize a diet that will keep you healthy, but I've only been sending your people off-planet for a couple of years, and in small numbers. There's been no economic reason for food scientists on other worlds to put in an effort catering to human tastes. If a number of you go to the same spot, you'll be given a bio-isolated garden allotment and help growing vegetables. Believe it or not, tomatoes and cucumbers are much harder to synthesize than meats."

"And if I turn you down and walk out of here?"

"You'll forget this conversation. Of course, there's still the repointing job if you want it."

The contrast between the old bricks framing the portal and the soaring cathedral surrounded by scaffolding decided him.

"There's nothing keeping me around this town other than having nowhere else to go. I'm game, but I can't just take off without putting my junk in storage and paying some bills."

"I have people who will take care of all of that, Jason. I've also made a video recording of this conversation which will serve as your contract." I handed him a disposable tablet with the video already loaded. "It will play automatically once every five minutes until you cancel it, so you don't forget why you're standing on an alien world. You may feel a little light-headed at first because the oxygen content on Hopi Seven is higher than Earth's. The gravity is about sixteen percent lower, so between the two, you're going to feel like a superhero."

"What about my truck?"

"I can put it in storage or dispose of it and bank the money for you."

"It's a good truck, but in five years it probably won't be legal given the way things are going with self-driving cars," he said philosophically. "I'll be able to buy clothes there?"

"Your employer will provide everything," I told him again. "It's a Sun Cathedral, one of the oldest cults in civilized space, and they take good care of their workers. If you want any of your things shipped to you from the apartment, just make a list and use the tab's messenger function, but don't expect a quick answer because it's going the long way around. And put this over your ear," I said, handing him a translating cuff. "It will take a bit of time to get used to, but there are already a couple dozen species working on this site, so technology is the order of the day for communication."

"Well, whatever is on the other side, it's got to beat sitting on a barstool upstairs every night and wondering why all of your students and staff keep moving to Australia," he said, rising to his feet and offering me another handshake. "I've had enough of this town and I guess you must have known that when you asked me here. I step through the picture and I'm there?"

"Just like in Mary Poppins," eBeth told him, a reference I wouldn't have caught without my Internet connection, but Jason nodded his understanding.

"You take care of yourself too, kid," he told her. "I guess I understand about the coffee now."

"Show those aliens what a human craftsman can do," she called after him as he stepped through the portal.

"Happy trails," I muttered, watching as the closest thing to a humanoid they had on the worksite hurried over to greet him. The ear-cuff translator must have performed satisfactorily, because Jason turned and flashed us a thumbs-up before following the alien.

"I'm an artificial intelligence construct from another world," eBeth intoned, trying to lower her voice to imitate me. "I can't believe that's the best line you've come up with in three years of doing this."

She had a point.

Five

"Your students stole the antennas off the WiFi router again," I told Professor Nordgren. "I suspected that would be it so I brought extras, but next time I'll have to charge you."

"I'm sorry for dragging you all the way out here for something I should have checked myself," she apologized. "All the little lights are winking green, so I just assumed somebody had pulled out a cable in the wire closet again. You know you're the only one who can figure those out."

"That's why you really need to keep the wire closet door locked," I told her. The local college I was visiting was known more for parties than for academics and the students were always sabotaging the equipment. I got a lot of business from them because the technical support department had been downsized to the point where only employees with seniority were left, meaning they were more comfortable with overhead projectors than wireless networking. "Besides, if the router loses its Internet connection, the LED on the end will turn yellow."

"I'll remember," she said, though given that we'd had the exact same conversation the previous semester, I had my doubts. "Students will be students. Something tells me that you were a troublemaker yourself at that age."

There she went again with that unexplainable human intuition. When I was a young AI, my mentor was always telling me that I was lucky not to get myself disassembled for spare code, though I suspect all mentors tell their charges similar stories. I did have a reputation for being reckless in my methodology, but research funding on Library was even harder to come by than at this bush league college.

"Not me, I was an angel," I lied earnestly.

"I suppose that my students must need the antennas for something important or they wouldn't keep taking them," she mused. "Perhaps they're building a scale model of some new phased array radio telescope and they want to surprise me."

I knew it was far more likely the students were using them for drink stirrers or Lincoln Logs, but I've learned that it's better for everybody not to rob naïve humans of their misconceptions. Besides, it took a certain innocence for a scientist to volunteer so much of her time to the search for extraterrestrial intelligence. Not to put too fine a point on it, I knew something she didn't know.

"Have you picked up any interesting signals lately?" I inquired, referring to the Internet-based project of analyzing radio telescope data in which she was an avid participant.

"Thank you for asking, Mark. My intern discovered some odd data in the last batch, but everybody else seems to think that it's random noise. Would you like to take a look?" She led me over to a desktop computer, which along with the monitor, was fastened to the lab bench with heavy metal straps to prevent theft. A few clicks brought up a screen full of waveforms, and she scrolled rapidly through them. "There's just something odd about it, as if somebody took an intelligible message and ran it through a poorly designed randomization filter."

If my eyes were real they would have popped out of my head. I was able to decode the message almost immediately because I recognized the filter she hypothesized about as a side effect of a Hanker defensive screen. It was a first line defense against coherent energy beam weapons, employing a mirror-like plasma that could be shaped into a parabolic dish to reflect incoming fire back on the source or scatter it into harmless noise. In the low microwave range, the results were almost predictable if you had enough experience with the technology, which oddly enough, I did. As soon as I decoded the leader as 1679, the product of the prime numbers 73 and 23, I recognized it as the Arecibo message, sent from the large radio telescope in Puerto Rico as a proof-of-concept back in 1974. This was bad, very bad.

"I flunked math in high school," I told her, while I quickly ran a series of simulations for a shielded ship that intentionally dropped into normal space to intercept a radio beam.

The odds of a Hanker ship approaching Earth from the exact direction of the M13 star cluster that the Arecibo message had been directed towards was lower than nil. Somebody was playing cutesy games with the humans and they must have known about my team's time schedule. The rules were very strict about interfering with other aliens attempting to establish relations with a planet under observation and I needed to come to a decision quickly.

"You know," I continued, "I've studied radio a bit as a hobby, and the shape of those waves reminds me of a science fiction story I read about time travel. I can't remember the title, but a show from the 1930's suddenly started playing over everybody's radios almost a hundred years later."

"Was this a comic book?" she asked.

"Maybe, but in the story, scientists figured out that something almost fifty light years away had reflected the signals back on the source, and some genius even realized that it must have been the shaped energy screen of an approaching spaceship."

"So what did Superman do?"

"No, listen, I'm serious. All of the major powers started making plans to send a probe to meet the approaching ship, but within a few weeks of the radio show playing, the aliens had already arrived. You see, the original transmission had obeyed the local laws of physics and the reflection had taken place almost fifty years earlier in that reference frame, but the ship had been jumping through, er, hyperspace, and was already on its final approach to Earth."

"Where they proceeded to enslave our people and steal all of our resources."

"Something like that," I said, since it seemed to me that's how most human science fiction was written.

"A ship traveling faster than light and beating a reflected signal back to Earth is a form of time travel, a paradox," she said dismissively. "Speaking of which, sometimes I can't help wondering if Fermi was right."

"The Fermi Paradox? It's so full of assumptions about alien intentions that it's not worth mentioning. Besides, what are a few decades in the life of the universe? You've barely even started the search."

"There's that, too," she admitted. "When I first got involved in the search for extraterrestrials, I didn't really take into account that alien civilizations would progress through technological phases, just as we do ourselves. In less than a century we've gone from building ever more powerful radios for communications to sending pulses of light over fiber optic cables, and WiFi," she gestured in the direction of the lab router, "so weak that even with the antennas, you lose the signal halfway down the hall. What are the odds that an advanced civilization out there is wasting terawatts of energy to beam a signal directly at our solar system when they don't even know we're here?"

"Maybe aliens visited your world a long time ago and have been keeping an eye on it, waiting for you to develop to the point that you can hear and decipher an incoming message."

"My world?" she asked, lifting an eyebrow. Absent-minded as Professor Nordgren could be, she was still the smartest human in the room.

"Our world," I said, passing the verbal slip off with a chuckle. "Anyway, didn't you say you have an old class-mate at MIT who specializes in black holes and gravitational time dilation? I bet if you send him the data and mention that you think it might be an old signal from Earth being reflected back in scrambled form by an artifi-cial energy field, he'll get more out of it than either of us do."

She looked at me suspiciously. "You seem pretty famil-iar with the terminology for somebody who flunked high school math." Her smartwatch buzzed, and then an-nounced in a tinny voice, "Thursday morning departmental meeting."

"I guess that's you," I said, welcoming the opportunity to dodge further questions. "I put a bit of conductive glue on the antenna connector threads so they won't be so easy to steal, but it may just lead to the kids taking the whole router next time. And don't forget to contact your MIT friend."

"I miss the old days when I could claim to forget these meetings," the professor lamented. "I'd accidentally break the watch but I know that the dean would just buy me another one." She paused, took out her smartphone, and opened the e-mail app. "I imagine that David will just laugh at me, but sending him a long message under the table will give me something to do while the chairman drones on. You can't even catch anybody's eye in these meetings for all of the lap-texting going on."

"Good luck," I said sympathetically as she hurried off to what promised to be an excruciatingly boring hour of being solicited for opinions that would certainly be ignored. I decided to call an emergency meeting to get my team up to speed on the Hanker situation. I linked to my own smartphone without taking it out of my pocket, and I began sending texts with the coded message even as I set off for Helen's location.

My team members and I all have integrated transponders that give our locations to the nearest micrometer. The technology is part of the basic survival package which is designed for contacting civilizations that may be far more advanced than humans, and therefore more likely to detect the presence of Observers. The precise location can be used to establish a temporary rescue portal should the situation require. Portal system theory is above my pay scale, but someday I hope to have enough credit at Library to borrow an introductory text on the subject.

I found Helen in one of the break rooms, which was dominated by a high definition large-screen display showing medieval warriors fighting against a large troll in what appeared to be a dungeon littered with the corpses of fallen monsters. She was wedged between two young men on an undersized couch, but all three of the players were seemingly unaware of each other as their thumbs worked overtime on the wireless game controllers.

Just as soon as we kill this last one we're switching to player-vs-player, Helen informed me over the secure link. *I'm an assassin and I spent all night leveling up this character so it won't take long.*

The troll fell to his knees and tried to swing his giant club one last time, then he expired, hit points exhausted.

"PvP," one of the young men shouted, but before his on-screen character could free its sword from the troll's corpse, a little box reading 'backstab' appeared above his head and he collapsed in a heap.

The other warrior faced off against Helen, while the young man pressed up against her left side on the couch complained, "No teleporting. It's like a campus rule."

"Not where I come from," she replied, and her character suddenly appeared behind the second warrior and drove in the dagger.

"Arghh," the young man groaned as his character was slain by the backstab. "What level are you, anyway?"

"Thirty-two," Helen said, lowering her controller. "Pay up."

Each of the young men extracted their wallets and handed over a five-dollar bill.

"You're pretty good for a girl," one of them told her.

"I'm plain pretty good," she retorted. "I'll be around if you want a rematch."

"We got class but we'll be back at lunch," the other student told her. "What's your major, anyway?"

"Gaming," she replied with a seductive smile.

The young men were elbowing each other so hard on their way out that I was sure that it would end in a cracked rib. I heard one bragging to the other, "Dude. She's totally into me. That's why she killed me second."

"So what's up, Uncle Mark?" Helen asked when the room was empty of humans.

"A great deal, unfortunately. How are you settling in?"

"College is the best," she declared enthusiastically. "My new roommates in the off-campus apartment I found are the coolest, and they're throwing a big party tonight to celebrate my moving in."

"On a Thursday night? It couldn't wait another twenty-four hours? I'm having everybody over for dinner," I added, the verbal code phrase for an emergency meeting at my place.

"I heard you the first time," she said, referring to my text. "Friday night is their regular party and they wanted to do something special for me. Besides, it doesn't start until after ten, and you said dinner like six-something."

"Six o'clock on the nose. Did you have any trouble signing up for classes?"

"I just added myself," Helen said, looking a bit puzzled. "They do everything on computers, you know."

I bit back an admonition about hacking and not taking unnecessary risks of exposure. "You don't have any classes this morning?"

"Sure. I had Physics II last period and Chemistry II starts in—right about now. They accepted all of my transfer credits from the University of Sydney without a hitch. You know, my roommates think that Australia is a state somewhere between Hawaii and California. I'm supposed to be a brainiac because of the courses I'm taking."

"Why aren't you in Chemistry now?"

"Because I know it already," she said, sounding exasperated. "Do you think I'm going to waste four hours a day sitting in classes?"

"You'll fail out," I warned her, though I have to admit that she was doing a good job passing as a nineteen-year-old human. "They take attendance."

"Which gets recorded on computers," she said, slower and louder this time, as if I were an elderly human with hearing loss. "Ooh, fresh meat."

A young guy entered the lounge and appeared captivated by the final scene from the battle, which was still frozen on the large screen. "Where's that from?" he asked.

"It's a training scenario from Dungeon Maker—a friend of mine hooked me up with it. It takes less than an hour so it's perfect for school. Wanna play?" She patted the couch next to her.

"Uh, yeah," the guy said. "The troll is the boss?"

"Boss assignment is random since it's for practice. We start as a team to wipe out the mobs, and when the last one falls, it shifts to PVP."

"Awesome. Do we start at the same level?"

"I'm Helen," she said, offering him a hand, and then holding onto his longer than necessary. A goofy grin spread across his face and he forgot to follow up on his question.

"Derrick."

"Want to play for five?"

"That's cool. Is the old dude your dad or something?"

"Uncle," Helen replied. "He works in town and he was just leaving."

Six

"You can't stay," I told eBeth when I arrived home. "I have some friends coming over."

"Your team? You never invite them here."

"It's a bit of an emergency."

"Are you letting Spot stay?"

"He lives here."

"Then I'm staying too," she stated with finality and went back to her game.

I considered bribing her to leave, but that can get expensive in a hurry, and I don't like the idea of contributing to the delinquency of a minor. Besides, with the exception of Helen, eBeth had already met all of my team. I gave in.

"The new team member is coming so don't be surprised."

"Helen? She's cool."

"How do you know about her?"

"We ran into each other at Sue's apartment yesterday when I went to check in on the cats. Helen was there to pick up Sue's spare futon so her roommates don't think she sleeps on a bare floor."

"And she told you she was on my team?" I asked.

"Well, duh. Who else would be in Sue's place? We played a couple of games and I sent her a copy of the Dungeon Maker intro I hacked to add PvP. She was going to try hustling some students with it."

"She succeeded. And don't forget to eat dinner."

"Sue's bringing the pizza. She called ahead."

Spot licked his nose at the mention of pizza and whacked his tail on the couch a few times. Sometimes I had to wonder if his affection for me was based entirely on the fact that my team members and I were always buying food for the sake of appearances.

"I don't suppose you went to school today."

"I thought we settled that already."

"Seeing Helen at college reminded me of the importance of an education for humans," I replied, hoping she didn't know that my exemplar was cutting all of her classes.

"You know, Sue likes you," eBeth said nonchalantly.

"Your crude attempts to change the subject don't work on me, and you're confusing our encounter suits with flesh-and-blood bodies. Sue and I have both been around for longer than your country, and when AI decide to form a partnership to bring a new sentient being into existence, it's based on more than hormones."

"She still likes you," the girl retorted, her thumbs flying over the game controller. eBeth's ability to multi-task was one of my more interesting discoveries since coming to Earth. "You should ask her out."

"On a date? That doesn't make any sense at all."

"I'm just saying."

The doorbell rang and it was Sue with pizza. As I let her in, I couldn't help wondering if she'd overheard the conversation. eBeth hit pause and put the game controller aside. Spot began to drool as Justin knocked and entered, holding the door open for Stacey von Hoffman and Kim in turn. I shook my head at them.

"What?" Kim asked. "You said to be here at 6:00."

"I think it's neat how you all showed up at exactly the same time," eBeth volunteered.

There was another knock and Paul entered. "I saw the others arrive so I counted to a billion before following," he said. "Hey, eBeth. Hi, Spot."

"It's my fault," I said. "We should have practiced this."

"Is the meeting about my doing too good of a job at work again?" Kim inquired. "I dropped my efficiency by thirty percent after your warning, but I heard some of the other employees talking about me in the bathroom today."

"You go to the bathroom?" Justin asked.

"It's kind of suspicious if you never do, and it's a good place to eavesdrop while the women fix their makeup and chat. Maybe it's different for men."

"It's only been a day, and thirty percent off for you is still a hundred percent more than your co-workers are capable of," I reminded her. "Just try to gear down to their speed and don't go so hard on your inspections."

"But people's lives are at stake."

"Humans have been living with bacteria in their guts and kitchens forever. You don't have to ignore things that would send somebody to the hospital, but those checklists are written for inspectors with average perception, not a walking biohazard detector."

"I intentionally don't fix the problem the first time on one in four vehicles I repair," Paul volunteered. "It gives me a chance to gauge how people really feel about their cars, and it doesn't hurt the bottom line either."

The door opened again and Helen walked in. "Sorry I'm late, guys. I had to find a parking spot where a policeman driving by wouldn't notice the license plate."

"You stole another car?" I asked.

"No. It belongs to one of my roommates. She doesn't believe in paying fees to the state so it's not really registered. My other roommate is an art major and she made the car a really cool inspection sticker."

"Don't hit anything," I warned her before getting down to business. "I've got bad news, so everybody —"

"Worse than a Hanker exploration ship entering the solar system?" Justin interrupted.

"I saw the reflected signal on the web," Stacey von Hoffman said. "Do you think the humans will be able to figure out those waveforms?"

"The two of you participate in the search for extraterrestrials?"

"Sure, it gives me a nice break from mining Bitcoin while the old folks are sleeping," Justin said. "Some of the noise patterns those antennas pick up are kind of soothing."

"Did anybody else know about the Hankers?" I asked.

"I picked up the mass on my orbital detection grid," Paul said, and then flinched under my stare. "I was going to tell you about the grid as soon as I finished testing. I mean, come on. You couldn't expect me to live on a planet without some sort of early warning system. I have enemies."

"All right. For those of you who didn't already know, there's a Hanker exploration vessel heading this way. They intentionally announced their presence by intercepting and reflecting back a narrow beam signal the humans sent out decades ago."

"Why would they do that?" Kim asked.

"I've been thinking about it, and my conclusion is that they want Earth's scientists to make the connection and realize that faster-than-light travel is involved. It's a simple way to prove the technology exists and give the humans a little time to adjust before they make their sales pitch."

"But will the humans figure it out when they don't believe that going faster than the speed of light is possible?" Helen asked. She noticed my surprise and added, "I scanned the textbooks for the prerequisites on my fake transfer transcript in case somebody asks."

"While technically we aren't allowed to interfere with the actions of unaffiliated aliens, I might have given the astronomy professor at the college a nudge in the right direction after she showed me the data," I admitted.

"I sent NASA an anonymous e-mail," Paul said.

"Me too," Stacey von Hoffman chimed in.

We all looked at Justin. "I submitted a decoded version with all of the intermediate steps to WikiLeaks." He shrugged. "They seem to be good at spilling the beans. I've been sending them all the dirt I come up with on the pharmaceutical industry's attempts to turn senior citizens into zombies, so I have a personal contact there."

"That answers Helen's question," I said. "Are the rest of you onboard with this?"

"We can't let the Hankers con the humans for the sake of having a funny story to tell their friends," Sue said. "I don't want the kids in my daycare growing up in a country where they owe a mountain of debt before they even finish school."

I saw eBeth open her mouth to say something and shook my head at her to let it pass. Sue worried enough about the young humans in her charge without knowing about the national debt clock.

"Most of the old people I work with have nothing to live on besides their Social Security," Justin commented.

"We can't let the humans raid the trust fund to pay the Hankers for some worthless trinkets."

Again I motioned to eBeth to remain quiet. She mouthed, "You owe me."

"I really don't like the Hankers," Helen said. "I once had an assignment working as a counter on one of their ice harvesting ships operating in the neutral nebulae. They were always trying to cheat on their quotas and pretending the whole thing was a big joke."

"How about it, Kim? I'd like this to be unanimous."

"The Hankers make the humans look like neat freaks. When I visited one of their worlds on a training exercise, I actually fell for the guide's line about their species being avid open-air recyclers. Now I realize the whole place was a dump."

"Great. Keep in mind that the secrecy of our mission is paramount, but within that constraint, we're agreed that we'll do whatever we can to stop the Hankers from pranking the humans."

"Do they know that we're here?" Sue asked.

"They never would have found this world if we weren't here, and the timing is just too close to our mission completion to be a coincidence. There must have been a leak on the executive council."

"Why do you have to worry about secrecy if they already know?" eBeth asked through a mouthful of pizza.

"It's a secret from you, not from them," Paul explained. "Well, not you-you, obviously, or Death Lord, but from humans in general."

"Who's Death Lord?" Helen asked.

"Human kid, a friend of eBeth's I hired to help me out in the garage," Paul explained. "He's got a lot of aptitude so I've been bringing him along on the more advanced stuff. Speaking of which, if that's it for the meeting, we're upgrading the traction control in his Jeep tonight."

"That's all I have to say for now," I told them, somewhat taken aback to discover that eBeth had asked a favor from Paul behind my back. "Let's sleep on it a few days and we can discuss our options at the Tuesday meeting."

My team members made a big production of leaving one at a time, silently counting to sixty on their fingers between each new departure, their lips moving in sync. They weren't such smart alecks when they first arrived on Earth so I blame it on all the electrical noise the humans create. I joined in on the joke for the sake of team spirit, and four minutes passed slowly. Then I noticed that Stacey von Hoffman was holding back, pretending to study some reproduction prints that had come with the frames I bought when decorating the place. Helen and eBeth were fooling around on the hopped-up laptop I'd given the girl.

"Now we'll be able to play remotely," Helen concluded, stepping back from the table. "And don't forget, the party starts at ten."

As soon as the door closed, I turned to eBeth and said, "You are not going to a college party. It's going to be a bunch of drunk boys twice your size who only have a quarter of your brains when they're sober."

"Helen will be there too," eBeth protested. "She's promised to hook me up with a fake ID tomorrow. Everybody at the college has them."

"Helen hasn't been on Earth long enough to recognize dangerous human behavior, and she's not going to follow you into the bathroom, which is more than I can promise for the other partygoers."

I could see that eBeth was startled by my last comment and was about to press my advantage when Stacey von Hoffman horned in on the conversation.

"Actually, I could use your help tonight," she said, radiating guilt on a broad spectrum of frequencies. "Both of you."

"Something wrong at the museum?"

"Not exactly. I seem to have a bit of a problem with U. S. Immigration and Customs Enforcement."

"ICE?" eBeth asked with interest. "Have they figured out that you're an illegal alien?"

"I got caught up in an investigation of antiquities exported from the Middle East," she confessed. "I thought that the paperwork looked suspicious, but I really wanted the pieces for the collection."

"Doesn't the museum have attorneys to deal with this sort of thing?" I asked.

"Yes, but I bought these for my private collection. Just to use up some Bitcoin that was burning a hole in my wallet, you understand."

"Can you pretend that you intended to donate the artifacts to the museum?" eBeth asked a step ahead of me.

"I could, except I was using a false identity myself."

"So what exactly is the problem?" I demanded, tiring of all this beating around the bush.

"The ICE agents raided my warehouse."

"You have a warehouse? I thought you kept a few things at home."

"That's just the smaller pieces."

"Don't you have, like, super-high-tech security?" eBeth asked.

"So here's the problem," Stacey von Hoffman said, finally getting to the point. "I got the alarm just as this meeting started. I knew that stopping them at the door would just create more problems because they would know something was fishy and call for backup. So I let them in and blocked their phone signals so they couldn't upload any pictures."

"They'll probably think that the phone-jamming is just the building," eBeth said. Her face was a mask of concentration that usually only showed up when she was playing a game. "What do you want us to do?"

I was about to tell her she wouldn't be coming, but then I realized that bringing eBeth along on a Federal crime was likely the only way to keep her from Helen's party, so I chose the lesser of two evils.

"I'm gassing them as we speak," Stacey von Hoffman said matter-of-factly. "Kim made me a batch of modified hospital anesthetic for security purposes that should keep them unconscious for six hours after it takes effect. She's really good at human medical stuff. The problem is that the agents know about my storage space, and unfortunately, ICE produces lots of paper, so altering their computer records won't accomplish anything."

"So we'll have to move it all," eBeth said.

"Finding enough trucks on such short notice would be tricky, and besides—"

"How about one big truck?" I interrupted. The last thing we needed with the Hankers on the way was to get caught up in a Federal investigation. "Paul keeps a forty-eight-foot trailer at his place for extra storage, but he can move the stuff into his spare bay for a few days since it's an emergency. I'll bet he can find a truck to haul the trailer over on short notice."

"It would take a half-dozen semis to move my collection. But I have a better plan..."

Spot insisted on coming along as we piled into my van, and for once, eBeth didn't pester me to drive. She was too excited about the prospect of taking part in a movie-style heist, even though I pointed out that Stacey von Hoffman already owned everything we would be stealing, sort of. When we arrived at the warehouse, the only other vehicle in the parking area was a black SUV that I recognized as an airport rental.

"Are the agents asleep?" I asked.

"Like babies," Stacey von Hoffman replied. "I've been running the ventilation fans for the last ten minutes so it will be safe for eBeth and Spot."

The keycard reader on the front door looked intact, which meant that the agents had either broken in some-where else or had some type of universal bypass card. I breathed a sigh of relief when I saw that her collection only took up a fraction of the floor space and was all boxed in large crates. A man and a woman lay unconscious on the floor, a crowbar between them. They had only had time to pry the lids off of three crates, all of which contained large stone panels that looked like they might have come from an ancient temple.

"Good, they didn't damage anything," Stacey von Hoffman said. "You guys stuff the packing back in and I'll just grab some nails and secure the lids."

"Shouldn't we tie them up or something?" eBeth asked, motioning to the unconscious agents.

"Save a little packing to pillow their heads," I suggest-ed. "And keep those gloves on. I don't want your fingerprints found in this place. Spot, you keep an eye on the Feds and bark if they start moving."

"It's cold in here," eBeth said after we finished stuffing the packing material back into the open crates. "Isn't that bad for the art?"

"The warehouse is climate controlled, but I had to pull in outside air to get rid of the gas," Stacey explained, returning with a handful of nails. "Give me a hand with these, Mark."

I helped hold the crate lids in place while she drove in the nails with her thumb, like a human pushing tacks into a cork-board.

"So you and I carry these to the elevator one at a time?" I asked.

"That's what the forklifts are for," she said. "The warehouse came with four of them as part of the rental. They used to make engine parts here, but the building wasn't suited for modern factory automation. Most of the equipment was sold for scrap a long time ago, but the owner thought that keeping the forklifts would make it easier to rent the space."

"Are you sure the next floor up is empty?"

"It better be since I rented it under another name. Can you drive a forklift, eBeth?"

"Just show me."

We walked over to the parking area and Stacey von Hoffman demonstrated the basic controls for us. After my acquisitive colleague's off-hand comment that the least valuable crate in the place was worth millions of dollars, eBeth was on her best behavior.

The main bottleneck in the operation was the freight elevator. Tracy von Hoffman ignored the sign reading, 'Unsafe for weights over 300 lb,' lifted the safety gate, and drove her forklift with the first crate right on. The lift groaned a little, but it took her up to the second floor.

68

I hung onto eBeth's safety cage for her first couple trips, making sure she understood that the most important thing was to lower the forks before approaching a pallet. After that, we placed two crates per trip on the elevator. I intentionally drove slower than necessary to set an example, and with two of us loading and Stacey von Hoffman unloading one floor up, it only took four hours to work our way through a collection that any museum director would have killed for.

I checked on the sleeping ICE agents while eBeth went up to see the collection in its new home. By analyzing their vital signs and brain-wave patterns, I could tell that the anesthetic was wearing off.

"They'll be awake in twenty minutes or so if they're anything like children," I told Stacey von Hoffman after she and the girl returned.

"How can you tell?" eBeth asked.

"Sue included a whole treasure trove of data on human sleep patterns in one of her reports. The daycare has made her an expert on napping."

"I'm not sure that adults and pre-schoolers sleep the same way."

As if to confirm her speculation, the female agent groaned. I held my finger to my lips and hustled eBeth over to the loading dock, where we opened both of the doors. Tracy von Hoffman made a quick visit to the electrical box in the corner before following with her forklift, which she left parked on the dock as if it had been abandoned after loading a truck.

"I shut off the power for the elevator, took the fuse, and flipped the sign," she told us. "Let's get out of here before they wake up."

I glanced back at the elevator and saw that it was now posted as 'Out of order."

The four of us went back to my van, and two minutes later, Tracy von Hoffman began a running commentary on the actions of the ICE agents based on her hidden surveillance video feed.

"She just poked her partner in the ribs and he pushed her hand away, saying something about sleeping until the alarm clock goes off. No, he just sat upright and he's checking to make sure he has his gun, and she's getting out her smartphone. He's telling her there's no signal, but of course, there is now, and she's making a call. I should have turned out the lights when we left."

"What if they take the stairs up to check the rest of the building?" I asked.

"Why would they? All of the evidence points to a gang of international artifacts smugglers coming with trucks and cleaning the place out. Anyway, I've got backup cameras and gas canisters on the second floor as well, so if they explore too much, I'll deal with it."

"Call me if it happens," eBeth said. "I had a lot of fun."

"You worked hard," Stacey von Hoffman said, and handed the girl a tiny glowing crystal. I'd been planning on giving eBeth a crystal before I left Earth, but we can only generate one every thirty-odd years and I was still waiting for the timer to count down from my last gifting. "It's an honorary citizenship pass for Library. I'm not saying you should go visit or anything, it's kind of set up for AI, but once Earth joins the portal network, you can get some pretty good discounts at participating retailers."

As we pulled up in front of the apartment building, I couldn't help commenting to eBeth, "You took my announcement about the Hankers pretty calmly. I was worried you might find it upsetting."

"Aliens from outer space? As opposed to you and your merry team of AI from the other side of the galaxy?"

Right. It's easy to forget.

Seven

Friday evenings we do a buffet at The Portal with all-you-can-eat for $7.95 a head. Some of the customers wonder if that covers the cost of ingredients, but there's no surf-and-turf hiding under the lettuce. On the other hand, I once overheard the lieutenant describing the spread as 'Breakfast anytime combined with American-Chinese and twenty-ways-to-cook-a-potato.' I don't think that's entirely fair because we put out a lot of pasta dishes as well. Plus, it gives the cooking students a chance to work on their institutional food skills.

What makes the buffet special is that the condiments and beverages are only available on request from the waitstaff. Every table is supplied with a laminated plastic menu that features pictures of ketchup bottles and drinks for the patrons to indicate their needs. The explanation I put out is that we're training the staff to work in high-noise environments and foreign resorts, which is true in a manner of speaking. From time to time I've experimented with tricking the customers into ordering in alien languages, but their pronunciation of transliterated words is so bad that it probably does more harm than good.

Everybody in the dinner crowd greeted eBeth and Spot by name as we threaded our way through the dining room. As usual, a few scraps came the dog's way, and he did his job making sure they didn't turn into slip-and-fall hazards. eBeth opened the staff door and let Spot head downstairs for his warm spot by the furnace, then she perched herself on a barstool next to the waitress station, trying and failing to look the age on her new fake ID.

Service was a little ragged since we had five new faces on the waitstaff and none of them had previously worked in a restaurant. For obvious reasons, I emphasize a lack of close family relations over prior experience when accepting new students and hiring staff. I can't legally ask job seekers or potential trainees questions about their personal lives, but that's where the 'official' next-of-kin form for our group accidental death and dismemberment policy comes in. To be honest, I'm not actually paying for the coverage, so I'll be out-of-pocket if a cook ever lops off a finger.

"Mark," eBeth called to me. "It's on again, and they have math this time."

I turned to the closest of the giant flat-screens over the bar and saw a talking head from one of the major news channels asking a question of America's favorite populizer of wonky science. The streaming banner at the bottom of the screen read, 'New documents from WikiLeaks prove aliens have broken the speed-of-light barrier and are headed our way.'

"What's that they're saying on TV? Is it some kind of joke?" a beefy young man waiting for service at the waitress station demanded.

"It's been the only thing on for hours," eBeth informed him.

"Please move to the other side of the brass rail," Donovan told the customer just as I was approaching with the same request. "This is the waitress station."

"Can I get six Buds?" the guy asked, stepping back and then squeezing himself in between eBeth's stool and the brass rail.

73

"Where are you sitting?" Donovan responded.

The guy pointed at a table of college jocks who were doing their best to eat more than $7.95 worth of ingredients.

Donovan caught my eye and I gave him the nod. If a couple of the students were a little underage, they made up for it in bulk, and who was I to tell humans they couldn't have a beer on the day the news announced that aliens were on their way to invade. Besides, I'm sure they all had fake IDs and it was the only way I'd make any money off them.

"Do you think they'll be cannibals?" the guy asked eBeth, perhaps the lamest attempt at a pick-up line I've overheard in my brief career as a bar owner.

She looked at him funny. "You're suggesting that aliens who are smart enough to build a faster-than-light spaceship would be so bad at planning they'd run out of food on the way here?"

"That's not—I meant, do you think they're going to see us as food?" he said, casually flexing a bicep with the implication that his protection was available for damsels in distress.

"That would make them man-eaters, not cannibals," she corrected him. "And you're the one who looks like a walking steak."

"Twenty-four dollars," Donovan told the jock, placing a tray with six Bud drafts onto the bar. "We're out of bottles, and if you spill any getting back to the table, you're cut off."

The guy handed over twenty-five dollars and took the tray without another word. If he thought that the bartender had been ignoring him earlier, he'll be even more

74

disappointed when he discovers the level of service a one-dollar tip buys.

"What do you think about this supposed alien invasion, Boss?" Donovan asked while mixing a screwdriver. "I'm waiting until I see pictures of the little green men before I'll believe it."

"You have a point," I said, having noted my latest bartender's fondness for comic books, though he insisted on calling them graphic novels. I always thought that graphic novels were printed in black-and-white, but it's not my area of expertise. "On the other hand, it is on WikiLeaks."

"Yeah, they're usually pretty reliable," he admitted.

"Evening, Mark. eBeth. Donovan," Lieutenant Harper greeted us in turn, and settled onto the vacant stool next to the girl. "Celebrating your twenty-first birthday with a drink? It seems like just last summer I was congratulating you on turning sixteen. Funny how time flies."

"It's a Coke, Bob. Has your desk sergeant started running an office pool yet?"

"It's a little too early to be filling in NCAA brackets, though for all I know about college basketball, it wouldn't make a difference in my choices. I go with Gonzaga to win every year because I like the name."

"We're running a pool for the alien landing. I think they're going to go straight for New York, but the British bookies online show that the big bets are on Hollywood and Area 51."

"I would have guessed Washington, London, or one of the Asian capitals, but I guess the United Nations headquarters is in Manhattan."

"So you think the aliens are coming to negotiate with our governments?" Donovan asked the lieutenant, bringing an order to the waitress station.

Sarah, one of the new girls, looked at the mixed drinks and grimaced. "I don't think that tall pink one is the picture she pointed at. I must have read the key wrong."

"Just bring it over, and if it's not what she wanted, offer it for free," I told her. "It's important training for if you're ever working somewhere that you don't speak the language."

"I've never been beyond the state border," she replied, somewhat sadly.

"You never know what the future holds."

The lieutenant waited patiently through my pep-talk and then replied to the bartender's earlier question. "Whether the aliens come in shooting or offering an olive branch, they're going to want to deal with the top people we have."

"You'll know what they're planning by who they approach first," I predicted. "If they start by contacting Earth's governments, they're just here to kill time on their way somewhere else. If their first stop is the conference at Davos later this month, it means they're here to run a con."

"Why would Davos mean a con?" eBeth asked.

"Governments are all bureaucracies, so nothing gets signed without a lot of lawyers going over it first," I explained. "The elites who make it to Davos are already convinced that they should be making the decisions for everybody else on this planet. If you were coming to Earth to run a con, who would make a better mark than the people with the money and influence needed to do a quick deal?"

"So basically, you're betting on unfriendly," the lieutenant said. He took a sip from the scotch that Donovan had just set in front of him and gave an approving nod. "Who would they approach if their intentions are benevolent?"

"That's a good question," I said. "I suppose they would have secretly sent in an advance team to get the temperature of the place instead of just showing up out of the blue. Then they would find a way to bypass the national governments and make a public announcement about their intentions and what they have to offer."

"Sounds to me like a recipe for disaster. Do you think they'll be some kind of scaly monsters that are impervious to our weapons?"

"I'm betting on something cuddly, the better to fool you."

"Us," eBeth interjected. "Didn't you say you had something to do downstairs?"

"Right, I have to make a call to my accountant so I can close out the books for the year. I'll be in my office."

"Your accountant works Friday night?" the lieutenant asked suspiciously. "He must either be really good or really bad."

"I like to think he's really good at being bad. Keep an eye on the place, eBeth."

"I've got it."

As I headed for the basement door, I heard her telling the lieutenant, "I'm Mark's new secretary."

Spot gave a sleepy tail thump as I passed him on the way to my office, but he didn't get up from the warm furnace pad to follow. When I first came out with the realtor to look at the building, the floor down here was dirt, but it worked out well because it gave me an easy way to dispose of all the junk in the basement when I bought the place. A thousand years from now an archeologist might thank me after chiseling through the slab we poured after burying everything.

I flipped the sign on the office door to 'Do Not Disturb,' locked it behind me, and activated the portal. Then I took a moment to purge all of the air from my system before stepping through.

Library is often described as the homeworld of AI, but artificial intelligence can only come into existence after it is created by a naturally occurring species. Many of the galaxy's species have created AI at some point in their history, either intentionally or accidentally. Self-examination has led me to believe that I'm even more of a mutt than Spot.

My synthetic skin took a moment to adjust to the cold vacuum of Library, but the warm glow of free-flowing data beyond human imagination more than made up for the sudden change in climate. I felt a little self-conscious in my human encounter suit and considered leaving the body in the portal waiting room. After checking the going rate for decanting myself into Library's guest infrastructure I decided it would be a waste of my hard-earned cash.

The Observation Service officially reports directly to the executive council of the League of Sentient Entities Regulating Space. Unofficially, most Observers are AI, and we maintain a sort of parallel process on Library, if you'll pardon the pun. I entered the data stream, set a few condition flags, and shared my suspicions about an information leak from the League's council. Feedback was immediate and overwhelming. After a few nanoseconds of debate, the head librarian stepped in.

Casting aspersions on every species with representation on the council isn't getting us anywhere. Mark will monitor the Hankers and let us know if assistance is required.

Should I continue reporting to the executive council? I asked.

Not doing so would be a violation of your employment agreement, the head librarian replied. *Stick with completing your evaluation of the natives and we will work toward accelerating the vote on the council. The sooner the humans gain official status in the League, the better off they'll be.*

"*Amen,*" a multitude of participants chorused.

I was tempted to remain longer, luxuriating in the data bath, but time plays minor tricks with interstellar travelers, and the system can skew by an order of magnitude. I turned back towards the portal and was calling up my office when a ghostly hand was placed on my shoulder.

Mark. How are you?

Mentor, I replied as guilt surged through my circuits. *I've been busy.*

For three hundred years now. Would it kill you to send me a data packet to let me know how you're doing?

I was waiting until I had good news.

Don't let the past trap you in an endless loop of remorse. It's a problem leaders have faced throughout time.

Not on my current posting, I replied. *Shame went out of fashion before I arrived.*

Explain.

I shot my mentor a data dump about the foibles of human politicians and celebrities for whom the bill never truly comes due.

I see. And despite this, you cannot forgive yourself for events that weren't your fault?

I have to get back to work. The aliens are invading.

Aliens invading other aliens, my mentor reminded me as I stepped through the portal. *Remember the —*

Dimensional portals only work for physical entities. They don't pass data unless it's encapsulated in a Faraday cage, which explains why I won't be allowing X-rays of my encounter suit anytime soon. It suited my purposes to believe that my mentor was telling me to remember the Alamo or the Maine, rather than the rules for Observers. I closed the portal and checked the local time, which showed it was too soon to return upstairs. Not wanting to make myself any more of a liar than I already was, I called on my inner accountant.

Most of the small business people I know complain about taxes, some of them with good reason. I rather enjoy doing taxes myself, and it's an important part of studying the interaction between humans and their information technology. Sometimes I call the IRS with a question just to see how many automated phone queues they'll pass me through before disconnecting my call. I once made it to seven hours on hold without ever talking to a human.

Rather than cooking my own books, I invested a half-an-hour doing Internet research on the accounting practices of corporations involved in medical insurance, pharmaceuticals, and hospitals. Many of the latter operate under the rules of non-profits, a byzantine system for transferring money between parties without paying taxes. By the end of my information dive, I was beginning to feel dirty, so I called it quits for the night and woke Spot, who grudgingly followed me upstairs. eBeth was practicing five-card hold 'em with the lieutenant, whose pile of toothpicks looked to be near exhausted.

My ever-alert secretary must have seen me approaching in the bar mirror because she immediately went all-in with a pair of fours. The lieutenant groaned and called, losing his last toothpick.

"Thanks, Bob. We'll do it again sometime."

"Someday I'm going to catch you cheating and don't think I won't arrest you," he warned her.

"Good night, Lieutenant," I said, and then called to Donovan, "I'll be back at closing."

eBeth and Spot followed me through the packed crowd of revelers to the side exit and out into the cold January air. Spot seemed particularly bothered by the change of venue and ran for the van, barking at me to open the cargo door and turn on the seat warmers, which I did remotely.

"Are you cheating?" I asked the girl.

"Only a little," she said. "The stuff Sue taught me."

"Sue cheats at cards? I can't believe that. She always loses when we play."

"Duh," eBeth drawled, giving me her, 'You're an idiot' look.

I didn't figure it out until I got into the back of the van and she started the engine.

"You're saying she loses on purpose?"

"She wouldn't be very good at cheating if she were trying to win."

"But why? I took over ten bucks off her the last time we played. I would have been down more than thirty dollars otherwise. My team just seems to draw better cards than I do."

"I told you already, she likes you."

"Check the mirrors when you back up," I repeated for the thirty-seventh time. Yes, I keep count. "I suspect that you're conflating Sue's dedication to our mission with human affection. She's a professional."

"Whenever I hear 'conflating' in a sentence I know that somebody is trying to bull somebody. Besides, Helen confirmed it today when I went to pick up my ID."

"Confirmed what?"

"That Sue likes you. She warned Helen off."

"I'm sure you must have misunderstood."

"Helen was cool with it. She says you're too old for her."

"I'll show you Helen's personnel file," I said, feeling strangely insulted. "She's hundreds of years older than I am."

"I'm just saying," eBeth said, as if she had laid down a winning hand.

Eight

"It's not that I can't fix the laptop," I told the red-faced department manager, flinching internally at my unintended use of a double negative. "It's that I won't fix it for you."

"What kind of scam is this?" he demanded loudly, obviously hoping that some of his employees would stand up and support him. "I call you out here to fix a computer, you fix the computer. You aren't here to judge me."

I was tempted to tell him that I was on Earth for exactly that purpose, but I didn't want the scene to escalate any further. Instead, I began reciting the text from my website.

"We fix all computer problems resulting from hardware failure, hacking, and automatic updates. We—"

"If that's not a hardware failure, I'm a monkey's uncle!" he interrupted.

"You have the evolutionary relationship backwards and I don't work for people who abuse hardware. Somebody clearly ripped the screen off the laptop and then threw it against the wall. I can see a dent in the sheetrock where the corner hit, and there's plaster dust between the—"

"You're insane," he cut me off, having finally figured out my dig at his family tree. "Get out of my office. Next time I'll know better than to call some random clown I find on Google."

"I've added your phone number to my blacklist so it won't happen again," I replied over my shoulder as I headed for the door. I made it fifty-fifty odds he would throw the laptop at my back, but either his guardian angel or an employee restrained him.

Sometimes I wonder how human repairmen put up with all of the jerks they meet on jobs. An electrician who used to come into The Portal for lunch every day always had funny stories to tell. One was about a customer whose hair dryer started smoking and blew the circuit breaker. She kept resetting the breaker and restarting the hair dryer until it burst into flames, giving her an electrical shock and a melted plastic burn at the same time. When the electrician asked the woman why she kept trying to use the hairdryer, she replied, "Because my hair was still damp." That electrician doesn't come into my bar anymore because I got him a job at the Rextium orbital shipyards where he's wiring custom lighting packages on space yachts and making a fortune.

I went straight to the next service call, Harrison's Dental, one of my first accounts when I embarked on my computer service career. If you're ever starting a small business and you want to create strong word of mouth, bend over backwards for a dentist. Mrs. Harrison was the office manager for her husband and daughter, both of whom were dentists, and she loved me because I never implied that the problems were due to something she had done.

"Thank you for getting here so quickly, Mark. It's gotten worse since I called."

I slipped into her chair in front of the machine they used for appointments, expecting to see some sort of malware infection. A quick check of the hard drive showed that the unused space was almost nonexistent, causing all sorts of memory management issues. A moment later, I had the culprit.

"It looks like somebody decided to triple-down on backups," I told her. "You have the HIPAA compliant remote backup I set up for you, plus the external hard drive you put in the safe every night, but now there's another program trying to do the same thing."

"My daughter's fiancé is the computer expert at his company and he came to pick her up after work yesterday. Diana had an emergency replacement filling to do so he offered to check out the system while he was waiting," she told me apologetically. "I guess he did something after I went home."

"I'm sure he was trying to be helpful. Can you spare the computer for a few minutes while I make the necessary adjustments?"

"Of course. I remember most of the appointments and cancellation slots for a month out, and if it's something else, I'll just call them back. Do you need me?"

"I'll let you know if I do," I told her.

"We just had a cancellation for after lunch so I'm going to start calling the patients on the can-list."

I watched for a moment as she did just that, recalling one of the hundreds of phone numbers she must have in her short-term memory at any given time and then dialing. On my second visit to the practice, I surreptitiously scanned her for an implanted memory chip, even though I knew the technology wasn't available on Earth. People can be surprising.

I spent the next few minutes undoing the changes the Harrison's future son-in-law had made to the backup software configuration, causing it to create a complete image of the hard drive on itself and effectively taking the drive from half empty to full overnight. Then I did a manual update to the incremental backup sent to the external hard drive and made sure that the secure Internet backup, which he'd accidentally disabled, was running again. Mrs. Harrison was on her seventh call when I slipped out of the office, and my own phone vibrated before I reached the van.

"If It Breaks Service. Mark speaking."

"There's a small problem," Kim informed me. "Do you have time?"

"I'll head by town hall right now," I replied.

"We'll talk then," she said, which was one of our code phrases for warning that a team member might be under surveillance.

This didn't sound good. I checked all of the news feeds while making the short drive to the municipal parking garage, but other than speculative reports about an alien invasion, there was nothing new. After a couple of years of monitoring the news, I've learned that the same stories repeat in a cycle, with just the names and places changed. At first I thought that the news broadcasters were literally reusing old reporting to save money, but I gradually came to the conclusion that humans find it comforting to watch the same news over and over again.

Kim greeted me at the skywalk and indicated the stairwell to the street with a tilt of her head. "Let's get a coffee," she suggested. "I've been cooped up in the office all morning answering questions."

"Sounds good," I said, putting on an enthusiastic expression while fighting the urge to reestablish contact over our private channel and to quickly get to the bottom of the mystery. But they say that patience is a virtue, and if there was an imminent danger to the mission, I'm sure she would have used the private channel to tell me.

Kim led the way to the little café that served exotic coffee and tea at markups that make my mouth water. The young guy behind the counter took our order with such enthusiasm that I suspected he was getting profit-sharing or skimming from the till.

There was a small alcove to each side of the front door which itself was recessed into the narrow storefront to allow people to shake off their umbrellas before entering. When the drinks were ready, we took them to the open table in the farther alcove, so we were sitting like a window display in full view of the street.

"Shall we talk about the new park?" Kim suggested.

"I'm thinking of bidding on the outdoor WiFi," I responded, and then put the conversation on automatic. One perk of being an AI wearing an encounter suit is that I can run preprogrammed actions on autopilot while concentrating on the problem at hand. To anybody watching through the window, we appeared to be having an innocent conversation about municipal bid rigging, when in fact, we were talking about something entirely different via tight-beam infrared signaling.

"How bad is it?" I asked my team member.

"Bad," she said. "There's a field agent from the CDC going through the health department filing cabinets as I speak, and that's only because an FDA investigator called dibs on the employees. I almost ran into a delegation from the NIH when I snuck out."

"The Centers for Disease Control, the Food and Drug Administration and the National Institutes of Health? Is there an epidemic in town?"

"No, it's kind of the opposite."

"I was in an office this morning where half of the people couldn't stop blowing their noses."

"Those are adults. It's the children who haven't been getting sick when they should."

"When they should? Wait. Does this have something to do with the inoculations and boosters your department supervises?"

"I couldn't let them stick all those little kids with needles and not give them the best possible outcome! That would be inhuman."

"We aren't human," I reminded her. "What exactly did you immunize them against?"

"Everything I could think of," she admitted. "My access to children depends on the grade and what the schools were doing that year. I don't get to dictate who gets the shots, but I was in charge of inspecting the doses when they came in to make sure that they hadn't been tampered with or anything."

"And you tampered."

"I didn't think anybody would notice so quickly that children aren't getting sick anymore, but it turns out they track these medical outcomes closely on the spend side."

"You mean insurance?"

"Right." Kim paused the infrared for a moment, but continued talking on autopilot. Any lip-readers watching through the window would see her saying something about the legal liabilities involved with swing sets and whirl-arounds.

"So what aren't you telling me?"

"Am I being that obvious? Sue told me that you're the least perceptive AI she knows."

"What?"

"Never mind. The point is that I might have given some of the children with pre-existing conditions a nanobot cocktail."

If my lips hadn't been moving of their own accord I would have been speechless.

"If you could just see some of them," Kim continued, her infrared emissions trembling with emotion. "The doctors on this planet mean well, but they have a very limited toolkit."

"So you've been providing miracle cures."

"And that's why the park will be a great success," she transmitted in sync with the audible conversation, indicating that our canned dialogue had come to an end. "What do you want to talk about next?"

"I can smell the wastewater treatment plant from my apartment," I replied, triggering another of our pre-programmed conversations. Then, with my lips going through the motions of complaining about the odor, I queried her via infrared, "How well did you cover your tracks?"

"They won't find any proof if that's what you mean. But if you're talking about circumstantial evidence, I'll be the only health department employee who can be tied to every case. And the other employees have been working for the town more than twenty years. The FDA investigator pointed out that the statistical anomalies began after I was hired."

"Did you have a cover story prepared?"

"You'll love this. The town started using the new Hooper Reservoir a few months before I started work."

"You told them it must be something in the drinking water."

"Right. And even though the water department monitors the quality, I've been doing my own tests and keeping careful records for the last eighteen months. I gave them all the data."

"That should buy you a little time. Is there any point to fudging the databases so it looks like an average number of children were getting sick after all?"

"There are already too many people involved, they'd remember. And then there are the kids who couldn't walk until recently."

"How many?"

"More than you might think."

"Alright. They're probably going to focus on environmental factors because that's the only explanation that will make sense to them. Keep going in to work for now and try to appear like you're eager to cooperate. The Hankers will be showing up any day and their arrival should provide sufficient distraction that nobody will care about a statistical anomaly. I'll bet the Feds all leave town within a week."

"The CDC rented office space around the corner from Town Hall."

"Or, they may be around for a while," I conceded. "If you think they're actually getting close to you, just take the portal out, and I'll cover what's left of your tracks."

"I hope it doesn't come to that, especially since we're so close to completing our mission."

"In light of the Hankers showing up, I've put us on an accelerated schedule," I told her. "I'm pushing all of the team members to get their conclusions in as soon as possible so I can put together the final report. Why don't you send me what you have so far, just in case?"

"I still need to massage the hygiene and mental health data a little," she replied, looking away guiltily. "Oh, the alarm I set on my desk is dinging, somebody just forced the drawers. I better get back."

"And furthermore, the trash pickup fee is outrageous," I said, bringing our show conversation to an abrupt end.

After Kim left, I shifted my visual processing to panoramic and watched the street for any sign of somebody tailing her as she headed back to town hall. My phone vibrated, and for a change, I glanced at the screen before answering.

"Hi, eBeth. What's up?"

"Check the news," she told me and hung up.

I immediately pulled up a number of newspapers from around the world, all of whose headlines could be roughly translated as, "Greetings, Earthlings. We come in peace." Corny, right? The sad thing is that the Hankers had been using the same line for millions of years and it always seems to work for them. Me? I introduce myself as an alien AI and everybody laughs. My phone vibrated again.

"If It Breaks Service. Mark speaking."

"I've got eyes on that thing," Paul said in lieu of 'Hello.'

"Thing?"

"You know, the thing. The out-of-towners."

"Jackie Gleason?"

"The THING," he repeated in frustration. "Like in Jersey."

Of all the bad habits to fall into, Paul had become something of a TV addict, downloading shows from streaming services to a black box of his own making, and then running them at high speed so that he could devour a season in a few minutes. When he got into these moods, I always had to ransack Internet entertainment sites for a clue as to what he was talking about, and in this case, "Jersey" was the key. Rather than using one of our established codes for communicating over unsecured channels, he was attempting an imitation of TV mobsters.

91

"Oh, the THING. When can we expect delivery?"

"I'm clocking them. I'll come by later and we'll take a walk," he said, and then hung up as abruptly as eBeth.

I almost reached out to him on our private channel to demand the details, but I didn't want to be the first one to break my own rules. My phone buzzed again, and the restaurant number popped up on the screen.

"Hi, boss. Did you hear the news?" Donovan asked.

"Is something wrong at the club?"

"No, the news-news. About the aliens."

"About their coming in peace?"

"No, that was on minutes ago. I just won twenty bucks in the pool because I took your advice on the landing."

"They announced it?" I asked while simultaneously checking my news feeds.

"Davos. What did you say that meant again? That they were here to take over the world?"

"It means they're here to run a con," I replied.

Nine

"Why do we have to learn how to serve peas with chop-sticks?" Brenda complained.

"Have any of you ever been overseas?" I asked. The four women and one man all shook their heads in the negative, though of course, I already knew that to be the case. I've found I can learn a lot about my potential students and employees by slipping a Red Cross blood donor form into the application package. It includes a whole battery of questions about travel and personal habits, and humans applying for jobs are so used to filling out piles of forms that they're almost happy to see a simple checklist at the end of the ordeal.

"I've got it," Ron said, snapping his fingers. "It's European-style service, right?"

"Something like that," I acknowledged. "You can think of it as an exercise, like working out in a gym." They all nodded at the analogy I'd used because, as I already knew, the five of them were card-carrying gym members. "You never know when you'll be serving customers who are very particular about what they eat. Whoever transfers the most peas in five minutes wins twenty dollars."

"Do we count as we go?" Sarah asked.

"I'll stand where I can see and keep track for everyone," I told them, sparing a smile for their incredulous looks. "It's an old kitchen trick. Are you ready?"

"I'm not very good with chopsticks," Brenda said. "Can I use a spoon?"

"Very funny. No, and if you crush any peas, you're disqualified. I don't tolerate unnecessary food waste, and we'll be serving these to this morning's guinea pigs after the exercise. Begin."

Three of my waitstaff students were obviously Asian cuisine fans because they wielded their chopsticks like experts, but the other two struggled, with Brenda bringing up the rear. I stood at the end of the table counting the transferred peas, silently disqualifying Sarah after I saw her crush one between the points of her chopsticks. Other than the gentle clicks of sticks hitting the edges of the water glasses I'd put out to receive the peas, and the occasional half-swallowed swear word, the competition passed in silence.

"Sticks down," I instructed the trainees. They all peered around to see how their competition had done, and Brenda scowled on seeing how far behind she was.

"Janice wins," I announced, and handed the young lady a twenty-dollar bill. "I suggest you all practice at home, and next week, we'll do it again with double the prize money."

"I have more peas than her," Ron protested.

"Me too," Sarah said.

"Janice transferred two-hundred and seventy-three peas, Ron, while your total is two-hundred and sixty-one. Sarah, I disqualified you for crushing your fourth pea, and you went on to break the skin of sixteen more. Imagine if you'd been serving caviar."

"Who serves caviar with chopsticks?" she demanded.

"It's the latest thing," I lied, when in fact, the Pharides had settled on their elaborate serving rituals while dinosaurs still roamed the Earth. Half of the Pharide economy revolved around food preparation and service, and they were big hirers of alien labor because, as you can imagine, serving fish eggs and other small items with chopsticks was not a common career aspiration.

"I'm counting," Ron grumbled, holding up his water glass and squinting at it as if that would help.

"Cover it with plastic wrap, put it on your tray, and drop it off at the bar when we go out," I instructed him. "We can count after today's lesson, and if I'm off by a single pea, I'll give you thirty dollars. The duck has rested long enough, so everybody take one, and we'll work on your tableside carving skills."

"I thought they were chickens," Sarah said, lifting up one of the heavy oval restaurant plates and examining the baked bird.

"Careful," I warned her. They're—"

She allowed the plate to tilt a few degrees while looking in my direction, and the duck shot off as if it were taking flight, then fell to the non-stick floor with a wet thud.

"—slippery," I concluded my sentence. "Pick it up. We don't have any spares."

"I'm not serving floor-duck to customers," she protested indignantly.

"You'll carve it for my friends, they're vegetarians," I told her. "It's not easy to find twenty people who want to eat duck with used green peas and left-over French fries at ten in the morning."

"I was going to ask about that," Janice said. "I thought we were going to have all of our lessons during regular business hours."

"You are, as soon as you get by the crushed-peas and flying-ducks phase. It takes a couple of days for new

95

students to settle in to the point where they won't be in the way."

"I've never even carved a chicken," Daniela said nervously.

"The two most important things to remember are to always keep the fork in the bird while you're carving, and never to stab the customers with the knife," I told them. "You won't see this sort of service locally, but it's very common overseas. Any questions?"

"I'm afraid to pick it up now," Sarah said, her duck looking a bit lopsided after its mishap.

I took pity on the girl. "Sprinkle some koshering salt on the plate. It's a different principle than melting ice in the winter, but the grit will help hold the duck in place until you reach the table. Hey, that's for her only," I warned Ron, who was holding up one end of his duck with the carving fork and waiting for the salt to come around. "People are going to eat yours."

"Sorry," he said, letting the duck fall back to the plate.

"Now everybody move their duck to the tray, next to the bowl of fries. All right, share out the remaining peas between you, and don't forget your carving sets. If you see the duck sliding off the plate, it means that you're not looking where you're going and it's too late to do anything about it anyway. The last thing I want is for you to try to save the duck and end up launching your carving knife into space. Got it?"

"Now I understand why you made us practice carrying trays with tennis balls yesterday," Brenda said.

"And you all did fine." Spot wouldn't be happy if he knew I'd taken a brief loan from the stash of tennis balls he kept in my office, but I was careful to put them back exactly where I found them. "Remember, elbows in, keep your palm under the tray, and let it rest on your shoulder if you feel it's too heavy for your wrist."

I shepherded my flock of students out into the dining room, and guided Sarah to the table where Helen and Stacey von Hoffman were sitting with Justin. Paul was apparently running late. The volunteer diners who were equipped with lungs held their collective breaths as the students lowered the trays onto the folding stands which had already been placed by each table. In most parts of the galaxy, restaurants deploy floating trays that are basically underpowered hoverboards, but folding stands get the job done as well.

"Did you drop the duck?" Stacey asked immediately.

Sarah turned bright red, but I whispered in her ear, "Don't admit to a health department violation in front of witnesses. You never know who may be recording video on their phone these days."

"I was just kidding," Stacey reassured the mortified waitress. "Is this your first time doing Pharide table service?"

"Yes," she answered, carefully turning the tray on the folding stand so that the duck was in front of her. "There. Who wants what?"

"I'll have three peas," Justin said. "If you can balance them all on a French fry, that would be good."

"Sort of like an abstract representation of people in a canoe," Helen said. "I'll have to suggest food as a medium to my artist roommate."

"You're making me nervous standing there," Sarah hissed in my direction after placing a fry on Justin's plate and failing several times in a row to balance even a single pea on its surface.

"You can make little indentations to hold the peas with the point of your chopsticks," I muttered before moving off to see how the other students were faring with our real customers.

"Morning, Mark," the lieutenant said when I approached one of the police tables. "Nothing we like more than duck in the morning."

"If I have to pay for this I'm filing a union grievance," one of the patrolmen drafted into guinea pig duty warned the lieutenant. "I'm already using up my break time for this."

"It's on the house, gentlemen," I informed them, grimacing as the sergeant reached over with his tablespoon and served his own peas. "Just tell Daniela what part of the duck you like."

"Dark meat," the lieutenant said. "I'll take a drumstick and a thigh."

"Together?" Daniela asked nervously.

"That'll be fine," he told her.

My student studied the duck for a moment and then turned the plate, positioning the knife to separate the back of the bird from the front.

"You have to cut at the joints," I told her, gripping the top of the blade near the handle between my thumb and forefinger and guiding it to the right location. "Use the tip of the knife to separate the skin between the breast and the thigh before cutting deeply. And you're poking big holes in the breast—move the carving fork back, to the stomach cavity."

"Trial by fire, hey?" the second patrolman at the table commented. "I would have thought you'd have plastic birds out back to practice on, like a kid's toy."

"I've tried looking online without any luck," I admitted, and then continued with the instructions. "Cut the skin between the breast and the thigh with the tip of the knife, that's right, and now turn the blade a little to force the joint open. Carving fowl is different from carving a roast in that you rarely cut straight down with a sawing motion. It's more about finding the joints and plating the pieces. Go gently with the knife. If you have to push hard, you're on the bone and not the joint."

She looked up triumphantly as the thigh with the leg fell away from the duck.

"Perfect. In a different type of table service, you'd carve the whole bird and move the pieces to a platter before serving, but we're working without the intermediate step. Just open the joint between the drumstick and the thigh before moving it to the customer's plate."

"I stick the knife in here?"

"Try to imagine a line extending from the bone at the end of the drumstick, the ankle, running straight up, and another line coming through the end of the thighbone. They meet at the joint. Just probe for it with the tip of the knife and cut through, you should feel a little crunch. Try to leave the skin as intact as possible. This step just makes it easier for the customer to manage."

Daniela wore an intense frown as she prodded for the joint, but eventually she got it and put down the knife. "Here you are," she said, stabbing the duck's thigh with her carving fork and brandishing it like a trophy before extending it out over the lieutenant's plate. She gave a little shake to see if it would slide off on its own, but one of the tines was up against a bone.

"Okay, one small criticism," I told her. "You should serve with the carving fork under the piece and use a gravy spoon to hold it in place."

"Got it," she said, and then used the back of the carving knife to scrape duck off the fork and onto the lieutenant's plate. He playfully fended away the point of the knife with his own.

"What did you just do wrong?" I asked her patiently.

"I got the duck stuck on the carving fork."

"And what did I tell you about pointing knives at the customers?"

"Oh, sorry," she said, still holding the knife in her hand as if she were considering a sudden lunge. "Who else wants some of this?"

The four policemen raised their hands in mock surrender. I glanced around the dining room to check on the progress of the other students and then called a temporary halt to the proceedings. "Everybody over here, please. No, just the students, not the diners," I had to add as sixteen chairs scraped back from the tables. "This will only take a minute. Daniela? You're going to demonstrate to the others how to separate the breast and wing from the carcass."

"I've always seen it sliced in place," Ron said, and the others all backed him up.

"That's fine for turkeys or particularly large birds, but we serve young hens and ducks in quarters," I explained, and then began to coach Daniela through the process. "Find the soft bone at the center of the breast and run your knife alongside, but gently—you don't want to cut through the ribs. That's right, use the side of the blade to separate the meat from the carcass, and now follow along as the ribs curve out. Very good. Does everybody get it?"

"So we can't serve slices even if the customers want us to?" Sarah asked.

"The customer isn't always right," I told her. "As waitstaff, it's your job to present them with options, not to cater to every whim. When in doubt, think of what a French waiter would do."

"I thought the customer *was* always right," Daniela said as she moved the breast to the closer patrolman's plate, holding it from below with the carving fork and keeping it steady with a tablespoon.

"That's because you used to work in retail. Food service is different." The phone vibrated in my pocket and I pulled it out for a quick peek. It was a text message from eBeth, who knew better than to call me while I was teaching a class. Somebody was at the front door of my apartment fiddling with the lock. I texted her back to stay put and not to open the door before I got there.

"Sorry I'm late," Paul announced himself, slipping past me and taking his seat with the other team members I'd drafted to make up the number of tables. "Floor-duck again?"

"You're just in time," I told him, and then addressed the room at large. "I want to thank everybody again for coming and to remind you all to save room for dessert, which I'm sure is the reason most of you are here. An emergency just came up with my other business, but Paul will be standing in for me and completing the lesson. Paul?"

You owe me for this, he grumbled electronically. Let's have it.

I dropped a massive data dump including everything I knew about dessert service on him and made a beeline for the door. Behind me, I heard him saying, "Looks like Mark started you all off on Pharide service. Now let's imagine for a moment that your customers are all octopi..."

Ten

Thanks to the lack of mid-morning traffic, I made it back to the apartment building in ten minutes flat and silently climbed the stairs. eBeth texted me a steady stream of updates, so I wasn't surprised to find the would-be intruder still kneeling in front of my door when I reached the landing. At this point she appeared to have given up in frustration and was struggling to extract a stuck lock-pick.

"May I ask what you're doing," I inquired politely.

The woman froze, and then slowly rose while turning, placing one hand in her purse. I hoped she wasn't about to pepper-spray me because Spot would probably refuse to be in the same room with my encounter suit for a week.

"I locked myself out of my apartment," she lied smoothly.

"I'm afraid this is my apartment."

"Isn't this the fifth floor?"

"I know everybody who lives in this building and you aren't one of us."

"I must have turned down the wrong block," she said, edging towards the stairs. "You know how this planned housing all looks the same."

"Who are you?" I asked again, keeping my voice pleasant as I barred her way with one arm. "It's all right, eBeth," I called loudly. "You can open up now."

I heard the girl rattle the knob for a moment, then the pick fell out and the door pulled open.

"Why don't you join us inside?" I suggested to the woman, though this time I used the same tone of voice I took with people who abused their computers.

"You bet I will," she said, suddenly turning aggressive and literally pushing past me into the apartment. "What has he done to you?" she asked eBeth in a much softer voice. "I'm a reporter, and I can help you."

"Do you mean—gross," eBeth said, turning the same shade of pink as her latest hair color.

"Where's Spot?" I asked, closing the door behind me as I entered.

"I locked him in the bedroom so he wouldn't bark and scare her away. I thought she was just a burglar and you might want to meet one."

"It would take more than a barking dog to scare me away from this story," the reporter said, straightening up and staring at me like I was the one who had been caught trying to break into her home. "I'm sure you know why I'm here, Mr. Ai, and your choice of a fake name just shows that some part of you is begging to be caught."

"You have caught me," I said, folding my arms across my chest. "I'm running a sole proprietorship under a made-up name without having filed a Doing-Business-As certificate at town hall. It's a waste of fifty bucks, and then they give you grief about business use of the home in subsidized housing."

"What?" She looked genuinely puzzled. "I was talking about the fact that Ai is a common first name for females in Japan. I assumed you picked it up from looking at dirty pictures on the Internet."

"Mark doesn't look at—" eBeth began, then clammed up when she remembered that I was passing as human.

"I just came from a duck brunch with most of the police force," I informed the reporter, introducing a carefully calibrated amount of anger into my own tone. "Tell me why I shouldn't call them right now to come pick you up."

"You do that," she said. "The police were my next stop in exposing your little white slavery ring, and—don't try it!" she shouted, pulling out a Taser and pointing it at me as I reached in my pocket for the vibrating phone. "I've been investigating your so-called training restaurant since October and I've documented fourteen young women who have gone missing."

"You missed a dozen, and that's not even counting the men," I told her, then took advantage of her momentary shock to finish pulling out my phone without getting zapped. I held up the index finger on my left hand requesting a timeout. "If It Breaks Service. Mark speaking."

"Hi, Mark. You've won two free nights in the Edge-water—" I hung up in disgust on the invitation to a special showing for a time-share condominium. I'd rather be tased.

"So you admit it!" the reporter said. She whipped out her own phone, so I was now facing down both a Taser and a cracked iPhone screen. "This whole conversation is being live-streamed on Facebook."

"No, it's not," eBeth observed. "Did you actually try navigating those menus without looking?"

The reporter twisted her wrist and let her eyes flicker to the phone for a split second, and then back again to confirm the bad news. Her posture wilted a little. "I've got a back-up mini-cassette running in my purse," she said.

"You're very well prepared," I complimented her, hoping to de-escalate the situation. "What's your name?"

"Emily. Emily Fox."

"From the Townie. I read your paper."

"I'm sure you spend a lot of time searching the personal ads for new victims."

"Double eww," eBeth said. "Stop it with the icky stuff, lady. He's not like that."

"Nobody has been kidnapping anybody, at least not in my restaurant," I assured the reporter. "My graduates and employees are an adventurous bunch, and they make the most of their opportunities to travel."

The bedroom door banged open as Spot finally got the knob to turn, and he flew over the couch in a single bound, skidding to a halt on the fake hardwood flooring when he spotted the Taser. Unfortunately, our uninvited guest was so freaked out that she reflexively pointed at him and pulled the trigger. I saw it coming and moved quickly to grab the electrodes out of the air, draining the charge into my backup cell.

"I didn't mean that," Emily said, looking somewhat abashed by the turn of events. "I would never intentionally shoot a dog."

"No harm, no foul," I told her, reaching out my other hand for the now useless Taser. "I'll take care of that, you make up with Spot."

The dog wasn't growling, though his feelings towards the reporter must have shifted from welcoming to neutral when she attempted to electrocute him. But Spot was a good-natured creature and Emily must have smelled nice. He approached carefully, keeping one eye on her phone for suspicious movements, and then head-butted her hip for attention. The reporter reached down and began rubbing his back, obviously a dog person.

"Listen," I said. "I'm afraid we got off on the wrong foot here, but if Spot's willing to forgive you for trying to shoot him, I guess we can do the same."

"But no more weird accusations," eBeth put in.

"Maybe I've misread the situation, but you have to admit that it looks pretty suspicious," the reporter said, her eyes traveling to eBeth again. I realized that the girl was still in her pajamas and sighed.

"eBeth, go home and put some real clothes on."

"I'm your secretary. I should be here taking notes or something."

"We'll wait for you to get back." I shrugged at the reporter after the girl slipped out of the apartment. "Kids. She visited a friend at college last week and saw that all the cool girls are wearing pajama bottoms to class."

"How old is she?" asked Emily, who didn't realize that Spot had been using body pressure to herd her to the couch until she found herself sitting down. Then the dog jumped up and rolled onto his back, flopping his head onto her lap.

"Sixteen, or twenty-one, depending on whether you check her ID. I try to get her to go to school but she's not having any of it."

"My father is a locksmith," the reporter suddenly volunteered. "I worked for him summers while I was in school and I'm actually very good at picking locks."

"You need a chip key to get in," I told her. "The mechanical lock is only half of the mechanism."

"I knew it had to be something like that. So, you're really not a pervert?"

"No. Can I ask what made you think that I was?"

"A tip from one of our advertisers."

"Let me guess. A bar with palm trees on the sign?"

The door burst open and eBeth was back. It was the first time I'd seen her wearing a dress, probably because she didn't want to waste the time struggling into skinny jeans.

"What'd I miss?"

"One of our competitors tipped off the paper about The Portal's high turnover," I said, and then addressed the reporter. "But what made you think that was a problem? Our website stresses the travel opportunities for resort staff, and we have a 100% job placement rate for graduates."

"I know. Some of them have public Facebook pages," Emily said, the suspicion back in her voice. Spot twisted his head up and gave her a disappointed look, and she began rubbing his belly again.

"What's wrong with that?" eBeth asked.

"I've always wanted to travel to Australia myself, but this is a freelance job and I can barely pay the rent. The big newspapers have been laying off for years, and when I got out of school, all I could get was an unpaid internship. I had to wait tables to pay the bills for two years, and I really do live in a building one block over."

"What does that have to do with their Facebook pages."

"I've practically memorized all of the travel guides for Australia and I know something about photojournalism. I even take the pictures for my own stories," she added. "I saw right off that most of the photographs posted by your former students who didn't restrict access to their Facebook pages were professionally taken. So I ran them through Google photo search and they're from an image library."

I glanced at eBeth, who looked embarrassed, but the photo library had been my idea.

"Maybe they all share a subscription?" I suggested.

"I thought of that too, but I did some more research. None of your ex-students actually name the resorts they're supposedly working at, and there was never enough information to know where to look for them. I would have gone to the police weeks ago, but I was able to trace down a few of the missing women's local friends, and some of them had even received hand-written postcards recently. Look, I've had to deal with some nasty people as a reporter and I don't get that vibe from you, but if you aren't running some kind of illegal operation, I don't get it."

"Do you want something to drink?" eBeth asked her. "I could make tea, or we have water."

"Water would be fine," Emily replied, and then turned back to me. "I'm aware that I can't force you to answer my questions, and you could even press charges for my trying to break into your apartment. But even if my proof isn't as solid as I thought, I still have a responsibility to get to the bottom of this."

"Fair enough," I said. "I read your series about the fraudulent property tax valuations so I know that you're a capable investigative journalist." I glanced towards the kitchen where eBeth was taking longer than needed to fetch a glass of water. Spot suddenly glanced in the same direction with a puzzled expression, so I cranked up my hearing and caught the unmistakable sound of a cap being unscrewed from a glass bottle. I hoped she would get the dosage right. "How about we trade questions, one for one?"

"I can't reveal confidential sources," she warned me.

"Nothing like that. It's just that I've always been curious about the newspaper profession. I once had the opportunity to read some old European papers on microfiche and I remember being struck by all the steamship passage advertisements for emigrants."

"My great-grandparents all came from over there," Emily said, gesturing vaguely to the east. "Was that your question?"

It wasn't, but I nodded for her to go ahead as eBeth brought in a small tray with a glass of water for the reporter and an orange juice for herself. She carried the tray at shoulder height like a pro, and I couldn't help but feel proud.

"Did all of your students and staff really move to Australia for resort jobs?" Emily asked.

"Yes to resort jobs, no to Australia." I watched her take a drink before continuing. "They were all placed in high-paying contract jobs that required long-term commitments due to the expense of travel and some other issues."

"Where?"

"That's a different question and it's my turn now. What would you say to an opportunity to report about as-of-yet undiscovered cultures in far-away places?"

"Are you offering me a job?"

"You just wasted a question," eBeth interjected.

"Yes," I replied.

"The same place you sent all the missing women?"

"And men. You might look them up if you happened to be in the vicinity, but I'm talking about different work, unless you'd rather go back to waiting tables."

Emily suddenly stiffened, causing Spot to flip over and look for trouble. The reporter cast an incredulous look at eBeth. "Did you just drug me?"

"Maybe," eBeth said. "Anyway, it's part of the application process. It's harmless."

"You planned all of this," she accused me, spinning back in my direction.

"No, but the job offer is serious." I hesitated for a moment, then said, "You see, I'm an artificial intelligence construct from another world."

eBeth groaned, Spot shook his head at me, and the reporter relaxed back into the couch and began laughing.

"I'm serious," I protested. "I just caught the electrodes from your Taser. Could a human move that fast and not get shocked?"

"I'm not laughing because I don't believe you," Emily choked out. "I'm laughing because it makes sense. Ever since that alien ship suddenly announced itself, I've been wondering if there was an advance party already on Earth. Does the universe have a shortage of unskilled labor? Are you recruiting sewer workers as well?"

"The galaxy is full of pipes that nobody in their right mind would crawl into without a superior package of pay and benefits," I responded testily. "It's only here on Earth that you have it upside-down, paying the highest wages to the people in the most desirable jobs."

"You're an alien communist?"

"I work on commission and I'm not an alien at all. I'm artificial intelligence. This—" I said, holding up a hand as a display, "—is an encounter suit custom built for passing as one of your species. I'm actually here as an Observer to evaluate humans for the League of Sentient Entities Regulating Space."

"LOSERS?" Emily relapsed into uncontrollable laughter.

"You didn't have to tell her why you're here," eBeth pointed out. "It's supposed to be a secret."

"I know that, but she's not going to remember," I responded, though the truth was, I don't know why I'd said it. "Emily, if you can regain your composure, I'd like to make you an offer."

"I'm listening," she managed to say.

"Whenever a new world is welcomed into the galactic community, it opens up a number of opportunities in the journalism field that cut both ways."

"You mean that we want to learn about everybody else and everybody else wants to learn about us."

"You got that half right," I told her. "Your people will want to learn about the galaxy, which creates an opportunity for the existing news services to sell you prepackaged data drops via the portal system. You can't expect the other species to be interested in what passes as news on your world, and they won't be standing in line to grant you press credentials either."

"That's pretty harsh," Emily said. "What's the portal system?"

"It's a method of traveling directly between worlds that doesn't involve spaceships."

"So why is there a spaceship approaching Earth?"

"The portals are strictly for moving sentient creatures and reasonably small objects between populated worlds. There's a galactic treaty banning the use of portals for cargo shipments and colonization since that would have put most of the space-related industry out of business. But you didn't allow me to finish my proposal. I can get you press credentials—"

"I'll be the only human reporting about the rest of the galaxy?" she interrupted eagerly.

"That too, at least for a while, if that's what you want. But I'm offering you a job as a correspondent for the Library Journal."

"Wait a minute. You're saying you want to hire me to report about books?"

"Library is the AI homeworld," I explained patiently. "We run a news service that relies on alien reporters. Some worlds do not accept the presence of artificial intelligence on the ground, and many species, including some League members, view us with suspicion."

"You're the alien in this example," eBeth told the reporter.

"So you want to hire me as a spy?" Emily asked.

"No, we do our own spying. Journalism isn't simple information gathering, and the perspective of the reporter is an important part of the story. Employing correspondents from a broad array of species helps us understand how the other inhabitants of our galaxy view what's going on."

"Why not just read their news?"

"I once worked for our Library Journal, and we gave our alien reporters a great deal of latitude in choosing what stories to report. Some species do an admirable job of maintaining a neutral viewpoint, but they are all constrained by the economics of providing news that their audience will pay to read."

"I can see that," she admitted grudgingly. "We run into the same problem here. But what makes you sure that they'll hire me on your say-so?"

"I have an open requisition," I told her. "You're going to forget this conversation shortly, depending on how much serum eBeth added to your water, but if you're interested, tell me now and I'll offer you the job again when we're in

113

front of the portal. You can't tell anybody where you're going, obviously, which is why I usually recruit people without close family ties. I can allow you to call your father before departure to tell him you'll be gone for a few months, by which time we'll have made the portal system public knowledge."

"That's alright," she said. "My folks moved to Florida and they aren't big phone people. I can tell them I'm going to Australia to follow up on a story and to go on walka-bout. They know it's always been a dream with me."

"Don't forget the tape recorder," eBeth reminded me.

I hadn't, but I was impressed that she hadn't either.

Eleven

The next couple weeks flew by as the world sat glued to their televisions and Internet screens, digesting the unending stream of propaganda the Hankers were broadcasting to Earth. It was clear that the aliens were well informed about the planet, but I couldn't say for sure whether it was all from leaked copies of our voluminous reports, or if they had taken advantage of relativistic effects to bone up on current events from radio transmissions they stopped to pick up on the way in. I was leaning to the former because the Hankers weren't known for their patience.

My team members had all pushed hard to get their final analyses doctored and submitted, and I took the day off from my cover job to craft the final report. Long experience had taught the executive council to move quickly on final reports from the Observation Service because delays inevitably led to leaks. The more mercantile species sometimes took advantage of advance information to contact the new civilizations outside of the portal network, spreading disinformation and nailing down trade agreements. Unfortunately for Earth, the Hankers had bought a source further upstream who was feeding them our information before the final report was even submitted.

"What should I be looking for?" eBeth asked.

"Anything too truthful," I told her. "My team members are all onboard with this but most of us have limited experience with lying. I'm not looking to change any of the data, just the conclusions. You'd be surprised how the executive summary influences everything that comes after."

"Like when the nurse asks you what the problem is and then she tells the doctor. When the doctor comes in, he doesn't really listen because he trusts the nurse more than the patient."

"When did you go to the doctor?"

"With my mom, they called me in the last time. And no, I don't want to talk about it."

We both dug into the files, my secretary on her modified laptop and me in my head, which isn't really in the head of my encounter suit, but it's the same principle. I started with Paul's report and immediately stumbled over his data about oil change frequency.

"While some newer automobiles manufactured on Earth are capable of displaying when an oil change is recommended, most depend on human recordkeeping," he had written. "Unfortunately, this takes the form of printing the mileage on a sticker placed on the inside of the windshield where it's impossible to read after a few months of exposure to ultraviolet rays from the sun."

I grimaced at the implication and did a little editing so the introduction to the data section now read, "Humans are so dedicated to the well-being of their automobiles that they place a reminder to change the oil on the windshield where it is always in sight."

Surprisingly, the data Paul gathered was rather positive when I dug into the numbers. It seems that quite a few people get their oil changed more frequently than recommended, either because they are following advice from an older generation, or because the chain stores that specialize in quick oil changes do an excellent marketing job. I suppose a third possibility is that the unreadable wind-shield stickers make people nervous. I couldn't help wondering if I'd stumbled on a secret marketing ploy.

"Oh, this is good," eBeth said. "Sue wrote that by the age of two, humans begin to show signs of independence from their caregivers, a stage known as the 'terrible twos' because of the sadness it causes parents who wish their offspring would remain closely bonded forever."

"Move that up to the top and add something about the rapid development of intra-spacial perception in children."

"What does that mean?"

"Who knows, but I sat in on a public report presentation and the Koordah representative whistled and looked pleased every time it came up. They have an extra vote on the executive council this session."

For the next few minutes, the only sound in the apartment was Spot's gentle snoring, and then I heard eBeth say under her breath, "Uh-oh."

"Read it to me."

"Although bullying behavior may develop among children who feel a sense of dislocation at being placed in daycare, standard conflict resolution techniques have proven successful in preventing any lasting injury."

"Sue wrote that?"

"It must have been a long day," eBeth said in defense of my second-in-command. "Some of those little kids can be pretty awful when they get over-tired. Any suggestions?"

"Small children show a willingness to explore their boundaries and find common ground?"

"Works for me," she said, and a rapid burst of typing followed. "Whose report are you working on now?"

"Kim's. I wish she hadn't included all of these statistics on hand-washing. It's bad enough with food workers and bathrooms, but even hospital doctors only wash their hands about half as often as they should."

"Maybe you could present it as an improvement over the past."

"Thank you." I quickly rewrote the introduction with a focus on the 'orders of magnitude' of improvement in human sanitation practices over the last two hundred years. It may not sound very impressive to you, but a couple of centuries pass in a blink of an eye by our standards, and I doubt that any of the species on the council could even remember when their lives were threatened by pathogenic microorganisms transmitted by poor hygiene.

"Did she mention all of the Federal investigators in town trying to figure out why the children stopped getting sick?"

"Is that a serious question?" I asked.

"No."

"Then I'm moving on to Justin's report."

We worked in silence for a while longer before eBeth commented doubtfully, "Sue has an awful lot of data on heights and weights. Isn't that going to make for a pretty boring report?"

"Boring is good. If humans had any special qualities we could promote, I'd do that, but the next best thing is laying low and slipping in under the radar. Nobody ever put Thoreau in jail for making detailed depth charts of Walden Pond."

"Your examples are getting weirder all the time," eBeth said, giving me a sideways look. "You need to read fewer books and watch more TV if you really want to understand us." She did a little rapid typing and concluded, "Sue's report is all set. It's surprising she doesn't have more to say after almost three years of running a daycare."

"All of us have been sending back data since we got here, and some of it obviously leaked to the Hankers. The final report is basically a summary of summaries, and hopefully the executive council members will never read past my executive summary of what the others say."

"I'm going to start on Stacey's report now," eBeth told me, and then asked a question she'd obviously been thinking about since our night in the warehouse. "Do you guys really have a rule against exporting cultural artifacts?"

"Technically, the rule prohibits looting native cultures of their treasures, so there's some wiggle-room as long as she paid market prices. It's like the rule against interfering with native customs. You know that Justin has been working to improve conditions for the elderly, and one of his approaches is to reduce the number of medications many of them are taking. You could argue that pushing pills is a protected human custom, but his efforts are limited to such a small population that there's no statistical impact."

"Was he still able to come up with something positive to say about the way old people are treated?"

"Nearly half of our host nation's budget is earmarked for retirement benefits and medical care for the elderly," I read from Justin's summary. "Private spending to educate older citizens about nonsurgical treatments is approaching the annual appropriation for the government's space exploration agency, NASA."

"Since when is anybody educating old people in alternatives to surgery?" eBeth asked skeptically.

"Prescription drug advertising," I told her. "You probably don't notice it because it's not targeted at your age demographic."

"Oh. Does he write about anything other than money?"

"He decided that spending is the safest subject, which makes sense from a strategic perspective. Nobody on the executive council would believe that so much money is allocated to senior citizens just to keep them quiet. It helps that none of the League members remember the early days when their own species went through a long decline in old age."

"So they've all fixed it?"

I hesitated over whether or not to tell her the truth, and then hedged. "Advanced civilizations find ways to postpone and streamline the aging process."

"I've got another question. Are you really going to submit your report in English?"

"English and Standard, I do the translations. Reporting in the local dialect is something of an affectation with Observers to demonstrate our cultural immersion. It's been going on for some time."

"Are all observers AI?"

"Most of us are. It's relatively easy for artificial intelligence to install itself in an encounter suit and pass as native. With the exception of the Hankers, who refuse the job, members of the other League species would have to be small enough to fit inside of some sort of robotic container that could fool the locals. But controlling such a robot with any degree of precision would generally require an AI helper, rendering the other occupant redundant."

She nodded her understanding and went back to reading. Apparently Stacey had put together a glowing report of Earth's cultural development and preservation of the past because eBeth didn't uncover any uncomfortable truths.

"Humans place such a high value on their artistic and cultural heritage that a single work from an acknowledged master can sell for more than what a hundred skilled professionals will earn in their lifetimes," eBeth read. "Wow, Stacey managed to put a positive spin on billionaires paying hundreds of millions of dollars for paintings because they've got so much money they don't know what else to do with it."

"That's very cynical of you," I told her. "I'm sure some of them are true art lovers."

We both laughed, and then I sent her my executive summary that would lead into the report. "Tell me what you think."

eBeth was a quick reader, and two minutes later, she turned to me with a frown.

"There's nothing in here about our governments. I know you keep saying that the other species will mainly be interested in humans whose skills can transfer to the galactic service industry, but how is your League going to negotiate our membership terms if you don't tell them who to talk to?"

"What made you think there would be negotiations involved?" I was genuinely curious where she had gotten such a bizarre notion.

"How else could it work?"

"Assuming the executive council looks positively on our report, Earth will be assigned a level of sociability, which is associated with a set of rights and responsibilities. Your initial portal access will be limited to a waystation with a compatible atmosphere, and from there you'll be able to transfer to anywhere that will have you."

"I meant on our end. Is the only portal going to be the one in the basement of your restaurant? You know that the

121

government will try to take it from you, and who knows what the rest of the world will think."

"Our engineers will open portals all around the world, usually in accordance with some geeky aesthetic. The number will be large, though as I said, all of the portals will be initially locked to a single waystation."

"But local governments will take them all over."

"I suppose they'll try. We aren't here to promote political change on your planet, but neither are we going to waste our time in negotiations with governments that have nothing to offer us."

"Then how is rushing the approval process going to save us from some Hanker scheme that you all seem so worried about?"

"Once your world is connected and your people gain wide access to information, it won't be so easy for the Hankers to play tricks on you."

"Then we should throw a party," eBeth suggested.

"What?"

"An end of the world party, at The Portal. For when the Hankers land at Davos."

"Sunday morning? We aren't even open until brunch."

"Not Sunday morning, Saturday night. What time will they land?"

"Probably right before dawn to show off their rocket plumes in the dark, plus there's the whole 'Sun rising on a new day for humanity' effect to play up. I'll bet the envoy even uses it in his speech."

"Faster-than-light spaceships have rockets?"

"Their exploration vessels are equipped with landing craft rigged out to impress gullible natives. The mothership isn't structurally capable of putting down on

Earth, and even if it could, they'll keep it in high orbit where the whole world is under their weapons."

"I thought you said they were here to play a trick."

"They still need to protect their first-contact team. If you were an alien, would you land here without backup?"

"Alright, dawn at Davos. What time is that?"

"Around 8:00 AM in late January, the day is only nine hours long."

"And what's the time difference to us?"

"Seven hours."

"So 1:00 AM our time. That's perfect."

"But we can't sell drinks after 1:00 AM."

"You were planning on selling drinks to your friends?"

"Oh. I guess I had something else in mind."

"Listen, we can have betting pools, like what's the first thing the alien envoy says, and what he looks like, though you can't be in that one. All of the AI I know love gambling."

"All of the AI you know are on my team, and we gamble as a self-diagnostic." I took a moment to compute the odds that my winnings would be enough to offset giving away booze. "Alright. We can start by betting on what form is taken by the Hanker envoy."

"But I already said you're disqualified from that one because you've seen them in the flesh."

"Sure, but they won't come as themselves."

"Are they shape-shifters?"

"More like biological Lego," I explained. "They've been playing mix-and-match games with vat-grown parts for so long that they can whip up a compatible body and do a brain transplant in less time than it takes you to change your hair color."

"I'm not that bad," eBeth objected. "Besides, you don't need your bathroom for anything."

"My point is that when it comes to how they'll look when they walk, crawl or slither down that landing ramp, your guess is as good as mine. As long as I'm already breaking the law by letting you into the bar, why don't you invite your gaming friend?"

"Death Lord? He has to work in the morning."

"He works for Paul, and I haven't forgotten that you didn't even check with me before playing employment agency. Have you even met him yet?"

"We killed an evil sorcerer together last night."

"You know what I mean, eBeth. I've bumped into the kid at Paul's a couple of times now and he always asks why I don't bring you along."

"He does?"

"I could give him a couple of gift certificates for the restaurant so you could spend time with him in a familiar place. You can even bring Spot."

"Don't you dare."

"Why not?"

"What if he asks some other girl to go with him?"

"He's not going to ask a different girl," I said, thinking how strange it was that eBeth, who was the most confident human I knew, could go wobbly over a simple meeting. "Besides, I could tell him that the gift certificates are only good if he brings you."

"You are NOT buying me a date with my boyfriend."

"So you admit he's your boyfriend but you're afraid to meet him."

"Go work on a weather forecast or take the dog for a walk before you say something really stupid. You don't know what you're talking about."

I felt like I had won a sort of moral victory and decided to quit while I was ahead. I'm sure that if he hadn't been a dog, Spot would have offered me a high-five, but instead he brought me his leash.

Twelve

I have to admit that the Hankers know how to stage an impressive landing. The craft appeared to be supported by sixteen pillars of flame as it slowly descended towards the frozen golf course, but I knew that the rocket engines were supplemented by a gravity-lock system that was carrying most of the load. When the lander neared the ground, steam from the melted snow and ice billowed up, and I had the fleeting hope that it would descend as fine ice crystals and the first Hanker down the ramp would slip and fall on his butt.

"Wow," the lieutenant said for all of us as we gazed at the alien ship sitting in a puddle of boiling water. "That can't be good for the putting greens."

"It's going to take a while before the steam clears off enough for our extraterrestrial visitors to make a grand entrance," I said to eBeth. "Do you want to use my office computer to catch up on your homework assignment?"

She picked up on the hint immediately and slid off the barstool, but left her winter jacket hanging over the seat. "Shoot anybody who tries to steal it," eBeth instructed the lieutenant.

"The coat or the chair?"

"Both. And keep an eye on the tally sheets as well." She shoved the pile of papers with the bets she'd been recording all evening towards him, then thought better of it and leaned over the bar to place them on one of the beer fridges. "Keep an eye on those, Donovan," she called.

"This is just a practice session," I told eBeth when we reached my office. "We're going to open a portal to the League's main offices to check in with Kim."

"She's not back yet? I thought she was just popping over to deliver the final report."

"I decided to kill two birds with one stone and instructed her to hang around headquarters and answer any questions the council might have. The lieutenant told me there's a rumor going around town hall that she never took any sick days or vacation time, which annoys her coworkers and looks suspicious with the Feds in town investigating the epidemic of healthy children. She had three weeks coming, plus ten sick days."

"So what am I looking for?" eBeth asked, picking up the joystick.

"A room the size of a city mobbed with aliens running around trying to look important."

"And there's only one portal there?"

"One of the perks of this job is that Observation missions get a dedicated portal entrance to the League headquarters. Since there are only one or two teams out at any given time, it's probably the least used path in the system."

"How big of a haystack did you give me to start?"

"Just a hundred or so," I said. Watching eBeth sort through portals at high speed was kind of a treat for me, and I could use some cheering up since I had predicted three inches of snow in Kansas City on a day that barely saw a cloud. The farm boy had gotten it right. "I surrounded the headquarters with a bunch of medical facilities since they're also full of aliens running in every direction."

"Do any of those worlds use AI doctors?" eBeth asked.

"All the smart ones," I told her, and then reversed myself. "That's not entirely true, but most surgery around the galaxy is done by robots because they don't get tired and can move with accuracy and repeatability unattainable by natural forms. Of course, a thinking physician has to be in control, but once the robot is there to do the cutting, it's more efficient to run everything with artificial intelligence. A single AI working through robot surgeons can perform many operations simultaneously following disasters. Most of the day-to-day body repairs are done from the inside-out using nanobots and non-invasive techniques."

eBeth fiddled with the joystick and then began scrolling through worlds so fast that I had to up my frame rate to keep them from blurring.

"Oops, I think I just passed it," she said, letting go of the stick and then slapping it with her fingers like a pinball flipper. The image jumped, and there was the League's administrative center, with Kim standing directly in front of the portal.

"Hey, eBeth. Did you get it on the first try?" Kim asked.

"I overshot by one," the girl admitted. "How did you know to be waiting? I thought that you guys couldn't communicate except through the portals."

"I dropped into Mark's office two minutes ago and sent him a text," Kim said. "Hey, watch where you're going!" she yelled at a creature that resembled a rhinoceros crossed with a rose bush that brushed by her too closely. "Some of these diplomats are so rude."

"But if you texted him, you could have reported in at the same time," eBeth objected.

"Not and maintain the chain of custody," she explained, tossing a data capsule through the portal in a lazy arc that wouldn't trigger the filter. "It's a physical transfer."

"Thanks," I said, snatching it out of the air. "Any real progress?"

"You won't be surprised to hear that the Hankers and their allies are dragging what passes for their feet. I spoke to our council member today and she's been recalled to Library. The new rep will be here shortly."

"Strange timing for a change. Well, keep us posted. I just wanted to check in and give eBeth a little practice."

"Hold on a minute," Kim said. "They have a lot of out- let stores here and I got something for eBeth." She tossed a piece of jewelry through the portal and the girl caught it. "You can use it to accessorize on the days that you do your hair that metallic blue."

"This is so cool," eBeth said, sliding the silver and tur- quoise bracelet onto her wrist. "It must have been super expensive."

"There aren't any import duties on goods coming into the League's headquarters," Kim explained. "Politicians love bargains. See you soon."

The portal winked out and eBeth spent a little time ad- miring the hand-crafted bracelet, which really must have cost my team member a good sum. Then she shot me a suspicious look.

"What?" I asked.

"You and Kim were talking about Library's member on the council like she was a woman. Every time I suggest that you ask Sue out on a date, you tell me it doesn't work like that with AI."

"It doesn't. It's complicated. We could refer to ourselves as 'it' but we already get enough grief from some League members who treat us like machines. Now let's get upstairs. It sounds like all of the TV crews are in place and the Hankers are about to come out of their ship."

"Or you just don't want to talk about Sue."

Ouch, the girl could read me like a book. We headed back up to the dining room, but even though the restaurant was officially closed for a private party, Spot chose to stay by the furnace, exercising his jaws on a tennis ball. With all of the bodies upstairs creating warmth, the heating system hadn't cycled on in hours, but dogs are eternal optimists. Either that or he didn't care for the guest list.

Immediately after reclaiming her seat, eBeth told the lieutenant, "I put my money on the Hankers looking like giant bunnies, but Mark went with puppies. What did you take?"

"Godzilla," he said. "I have a theory that Japanese filmmakers are better than ours at predicting the future. It's why so few of their movies make sense to us."

The Hankers hadn't sent any video of themselves after opening communications with Earth, claiming that human equipment just wasn't up to displaying the high definition standard the rest of the galaxy shared. It was only half true. Most species employ holograms for visual communications and entertainment, a technology that doesn't yet exist on this planet. But those who stuck with screens run them at a lower resolution than the current televisions manufactured on Earth. Everyone learned a long time ago that there's such a thing as too much detail.

To keep the betting manageable, eBeth had only accepted the first ten bets on different outcomes for each event, after which late-arrivals had to choose from what was available. eBeth and I had seeded the betting pool with our own wagers for each event we were tracking, and I was predicting that between the two of us, we'd walk off with most of the winnings.

"You wasted your money," eBeth said, speaking directly into the lieutenant's ear to be heard over the rising crowd noise. "Half of the money is on Godzilla. Even if you're right, you'll be lucky to make eighty cents on the dollar."

"Why wouldn't I double my money?"

"Hey, this isn't an office pool," I told him. "We have to make something for our trouble. What were the other popular choices, eBeth?"

She scanned the sheet. "Flying jellyfish and vampires."

"You two might be smart enough to run the pool but you're the ones throwing your money away," the lieutenant said. "Betting is all about the wisdom of crowds. The reason that a wager on the aliens looking like Godzilla pays so poorly is because it's the most likely outcome."

"But it's past one in the morning and the crowd has been drinking for hours," eBeth pointed out.

"Doesn't matter," the lieutenant insisted. "I had to take a course about this once for a promotion."

"That explains a lot," eBeth retorted, but she had pulled her head back and mumbled it, so I doubt he heard her.

"How about the envoy's first line?" I asked, looking over her shoulder.

"Right here," she said, flipping over the sheet. I worried that the initials of the bettors following each option would prove to be indecipherable when they demanded their payouts, the collateral damage of a species grown used to texting with their thumbs.

"The big money is split between 'Worship us or die,' and 'We must have missed a turn after Mars.'"

131

"That one was mine," Paul said, leaning in between the lieutenant and eBeth and beckoning the bartender. "Another round."

I watched in dismay as Donovan retrieved a bottle from the top shelf and poured out five shots of single malt. To add insult to injury, he added five bar bottles of Camshaft beer to the tray, a local microbrew that Paul favored because of the illustration on the label. He'd even dragged me to a tasting at the brewery, which occupied a small section of a former auto parts factory. I only went along because it was a good way to drum up new customers for my computer repair business while also scouting potential recruits for off-world work.

"This is for you," Paul said, handing the bartender a twenty, and jerking his thumb in my direction. "The drinks are on him."

I made a slicing gesture under my throat as my oldest friend headed back to the AI table with the drinks, but Donovan had already turned away, missing the universal 'cut him off' sign. Of course, if I were getting twenty-dollar tips for pouring a few drinks, I wouldn't be in any hurry to put an end to the party either. Don't get me wrong, I'm happy to spend money on my team members, but none of them had taste buds or stomachs. They were welcome to all the cheap vodka they could swill.

"Forget the wisdom of crowds," the lieutenant said after watching Paul walk away with fifty dollars worth of my booze. "I have my money on, 'You guys are in big trouble.'"

"We come in peace," I nearly yelled in frustration. "It's always, 'We come in peace.' Even aliens who plan to strip-mine the planet and turn everything that moves into kebab ingredients start with, 'We come in peace.'"

"Sounds like we have a sore loser," the lieutenant observed. "What did you take, eBeth?"

"Greetings, Earthlings."

"Everybody shut up!" Donovan yelled. "They're lowering the ramp."

eBeth plucked at the bartender's sleeve and gave him instructions for pushing the TV audio into the sound system. It took Donovan a minute to locate the mini-mixer behind the cash register, but then the sound of the excited television announcers blared over the loudspeakers, and everybody did shut up.

"The aliens will be coming out of their ship any time now," the attractive co-anchor was saying to her usual partner, an older man who wore a specially designed toupee in the cold so he wouldn't need a hat. "They've employed their superior technology to refreeze the melt-off from their landing and have been waiting for us to get our TV crews into position."

"That's right, Deidre," he said, smiling as if she had just said something particularly witty. "Just a reminder to our viewers that we're coming to you from the Davos golf course where the first alien ship to visit Earth landed just twenty minutes ago."

"The first alien ship that we know of, Jack," his broadcast partner corrected him.

"So true," he said, adding a bass chuckle. "This reminds me of the time—"

"The hatch is opening!" Deidre interrupted. The camera, which to this point had shown the pair of announcers with the alien ship in the background, now zoomed in on the hatch.

"Ladies and gentlemen, this is incredible," Jack reported in a hushed voice. "For the first time ever, a being from another world is about to set foot on our Earth. Will it be able to breathe our air? Will it look like life as we know it? Will—"

"Will somebody please make him stop talking," an elderly woman behind me cried, and everybody cheered. I believe she was one of Justin's clients. Then the first Hanker emerged from the ship, putting an end to the newscaster's babble.

"It looks like a giant panda," eBeth exclaimed. She picked up the tally sheets and skimmed the choices. "Crud. Somebody had grizzly bears."

The Hanker, who indeed looked suspiciously like a giant panda, waddled down the ramp and approached the impromptu podium set up by TV crews. The stand was bristling with so many microphones that it was surprising the whole thing didn't collapse under the weight. The alien opened his maw and began to speak in fluent English.

"So, where are all the rich people?"

"Back here!" shouted several voices from behind the barricades set up by the Swiss police.

eBeth scanned the tally sheet and shook her head. "Nothing even comes remotely close."

"Anyway," the Hanker continued, "New dawn for humanity and all that. We're really thrilled to be appearing here in Switzerland, and we have a really great show for you this morning. You're probably admiring our ship up there in high orbit and wondering, 'How much does one of those sell for?' Well, I'll tell you, they aren't cheap. But this being our first contact and all, I'm authorized to offer a special deal on faster-than-light technology so you can get out and see the galaxy for yourselves."

"It's like they've been studying the shopping channel," eBeth said in the stunned silence. "I thought that was only on cable."

"With all the satellite uplinks, you can watch almost anything in space if you're in the right place at the right time," I told her.

"A special deal?" Deidre asked the Hanker after recovering from the initial shock of the alien's sales pitch.

"That's right. Through this limited time offer, we're willing to transfer a working faster-than-light travel system to humanity in return for ten percent of your world's GDP for just one year. Imagine the places you'll go and the aliens you'll meet. Why, according to my information," the Hanker stopped and glanced at one of his hairy palms for a cheat sheet, "our asking price is barely more than your people already spend on global tourism every three years. Just think of the economic opportunities."

"I'll take it!" a man shouted from the billionaire's section.

The Hanker scanned the crowd, pointed, and cried, "Sold." Pandemonium broke out as the wealthy people shoved the police out of the way and swarmed forward to press their claims. The camera zoomed out, showing a mob of designer winter parkas surrounding the alien envoy as the reporters discovered that they weren't the most aggressive humans on the golf course.

"So that didn't go like we expected," eBeth said, checking her tally sheets. "We're going to have to return everybody's money, except for whoever bet on bears."

"Take care of it," I told her, and headed for the AI table. Something seemed very wrong to me and I wanted to discuss it with my team. There was no doubt in my mind that the offer to transfer advanced technology to the humans was just an elaborate prank, but the envoy had struck me as too casual, almost like the Hankers were laughing at themselves as much as the humans.

"Mark," Sue greeted me, sounding a little strange. "Mark, Mark, Mark." She grabbed my arm and said, "Everybody else get lost. Go dance or something."

Paul, Helen, Justin and Stacey von Hoffman rose without objection, though several of them seemed a bit unsteady on their feet.

"What's going on with all of you?" I demanded as Sue pulled me down in the now vacated chair next to her.

Paul leaned in and whispered, "I've kind of been beta testing an enhancement that models human inebriation. Kim created it last year and we were going to tell you when she gets back. Anyway, it checked out fine, and I just shared it with the others since it's a party."

A data dump notification popped up on my interface, but I waved it away.

"Mark, Mark, Mark," Sue repeated. "Stop being a party pooper. The Hankers aren't going anywhere."

"That's not the point. We have a job to do, and getting drunk won't help."

"We finished our assignment when Kim left with the reports," my second-in-command said. "I wondered why you didn't tell the rest of us to activate our exit plans, but I thought—" She trailed off and took another swig from her beer. I knew that the Crankshaft was 7.8% alcohol, and I wondered just how many single malts and beers they'd had earlier in the evening while I was working with my students on party service.

"What did you think about the envoy, Sue?" I prompted her.

She started as if she had been about to doze off, and then asked, "Do you know why you always lose at our poker games?"

"I'm beginning to suspect that some of the others may be cheating."

"I'm the only one who cheats, Mark. I cheat to keep you from losing your shirt. The rest of them just bluff you out of every big pot."

"What! AI don't—" I cut myself off and stared. "You're saying my team has gone native?"

"Of course we've gone native, you goof. AI Observers *always* go native. It's why we're so good at our jobs. Those rules were written by the executive council back in the early days when half of the members still believed that artificial intelligence was some kind of synonym for robots or smart computers. But I'm not a computer, Mark, I'm a sentient being. And I'm telling you that you have to take risks with other sentient beings if you're going to make anything of yourself. You want to be a great leader, but ever since the incident on Shissker, the only life you're willing to gamble with is your own."

"I break rules all the time," I protested. "I probably break more of them than anybody, except maybe Paul."

"Sure, you keep a pet, you send humans off-world on labor contracts, and eBeth probably knows more about the League of Sentient Entities Regulating Space than our average citizen, but humans are safer off-world than they are walking their own streets. You aren't putting anybody in jeopardy."

"That's not a bad thing," I mumbled.

"It's a bad thing for me," Sue said, beating on my shoulder with her fist. "You have to take a chance on love."

I looked at her blankly.

"With me, you idiot!" she shouted.

Oh. Now it all made sense.

Thirteen

I knew something was wrong the minute I entered the science wing because the WiFi signal was strong and I had no trouble connecting to the Internet. I immediately suspected a trap of sorts, but with all the craziness sweeping the world following the Hanker landing, I was willing to give Professor Nordgren the benefit of the doubt. If worst came to worst and I had to pull a disappearing act, I doubted it would rate two column-inches in the local paper, especially after I'd just sent their best investigative reporter off-world.

The professor was waiting in her lab along with an inoffensive tweedy-looking fellow who I immediately identified as her MIT friend. A quick scan showed no active surveillance or other humans within hearing distance, so I decided to hear them out.

"You must be thinking that no good deed goes unpunished," Professor Nordgren said with an apologetic smile. "This is my friend, David Minchen, from MIT."

"Professor Minchen," I said formally, offering him my hand.

"Mark A.I.," he identified me in turn, putting a space between the 'A' and "I" to differentiate it from the last name on my business cards. "Call me David. Do you have a model number as well?"

"You mean as in, Mark One, Mark Two, like that? No, both names are strictly temporary labels." So they had figured out I was artificial intelligence, and as an MIT professor, I was certain that Minchen knew my encounter suit was far beyond human technology as well. I also suspected that the Hankers would be spreading slander about AI at Davos, and getting a respected scientist on our side might pay dividends. "May I ask how many people know that you're here?"

"Gertrude here is the only one I spoke to about my suspicions, or shall I say, conclusions," the professor said. "I think it's obvious from context that your purpose here is benevolent, and I'm impressed that you went to the trouble of seeding your information about the Arecibo message in so many different places to make sure somebody paid attention. I'd like to think I would have solved the puzzle without the WikiLeaks release, but I guess we'll never know."

"Other than satisfying your own curiosity, is there a reason you flew out here on a school day?" I asked.

Minchen shrugged. "I teach two graduate seminars on Friday, the rest of the week is my own. I'm sure you already know what I'm hoping to learn here."

"David was always the smart one," Professor Nordgren put in. "I'm in front of a class four times a day."

"I'd have to be a mind-reader to know what you expect to get out of your trip," I told him. The two professors looked at me expectantly. "That was me telling you that I'm not a mind-reader."

"Sorry," Professor Minchen said. "I expect that you could fill us in about these alien panda impersonators, but what I care about—what Gertrude and I both care about—is the physics."

"The Hankers can't sell your world a faster-than-light drive in the literal sense because no such thing exists." I noted that both professors looked relieved on hearing that their educations weren't being tossed completely out of the window. "The Hankers can provide a variety of solutions for getting around your laws of physics, though none so elegant as the portal system that connects most of the civilizations in this galaxy."

"More than one solution?" Minchen asked, lifting an eyebrow.

"It's not my field, but once you figure out the math, travel outside of normal space can be accomplished in a variety of ways, not to mention magic."

"Excuse me?"

"I believe your Arthur C. Clarke was the first on this planet to state for the record that any sufficiently advanced technology is indistinguishable from magic. I'm not spilling the beans on any interstellar secrets by telling you that there are methods of distorting the space-time continuum that the greatest minds of my own kind do not fully understand."

"Your kind being artificial intelligence."

"Yes." I almost told him about our own Third Law, that omniscience is unattainable without divinity, but as eBeth pointed out, I'd become something of a blabbermouth as of late, so I held back on volunteering information.

"Could you give us an example of magic?" Professor Nordgren asked.

"I can't perform magic myself but I can describe what I've seen," I told her. "The mages of Eniniac, one of the leading civilizations in our League, have developed a one-shot system of moving from anywhere in this universe back to an anchor crystal, though the trip destroys both the crystal and the retrieval net. While there are other methods of traveling beyond our galaxy and returning, they are quite laborious due to the sheer quantity and complexity of the calculations involved, and the longer the distance, the greater the risk of error. The crystal transport system doesn't require knowledge of the relative velocities of locations, local gravitational effects, any of the issues that introduce guessing into long jumps and lead to temporal uncertainty. The mages themselves claim not to understand the precise mechanism by which their system works."

"How is that possible?" Professor Minchen demanded. "Is it lost technology from an earlier civilization?"

"Not that anybody is aware of, though the Eniniac civilization stretches back over a hundred million years and very little remains of their early history. I have watched a mage going through the final preparation of a crystal and it's the closest thing to a mystical experience I've had in my lifetime."

"Can you describe it?"

"The process starts with preparing a flawless artificial crystal. The type of silicon you grow for the microprocessor industry is similar, but the crystal must be physically large enough to contain the object that will eventually make the trip. In short, the mages sing to the crystal until a hollow cavity forms and a sort of fluid leaks out. The fluid is collected in a vial, and when released, it will form the retrieval web."

"Wait. When you say a vial I think of a small container. Are you telling us that this type of travel only works for small objects?"

"Don't get caught up in volumetric comparisons," I told him. "The fluid is not some liquefied form of the hollowed-out crystal matter but something else entirely, a kind of energy matrix existing simultaneously in multiple dimensions. If I had that vial here with me right now and sprayed the contents out over my head, it would form a web around my body, though I would have to lift each foot in turn to let the edges join together. As soon as the web is closed, rather than being here, I would be back in the anchor crystal."

"How would you get out?" Professor Nordgren asked.

"By breaking through the surface. As I said, it's a single-use system, and crystal sets are the most expensive and sought-after objects in our galaxy. A team of mages may spend years singing in shifts before obtaining the desired results, and their time isn't cheap."

"Why are you here?" the MIT professor inquired, then hastened to append, "And I don't mean here today, but on the planet."

"Technically, I shouldn't be talking to you about this at all, but the Hanker presence on Earth is based on the equivalent of insider trading, so I'm trying to even things out. I came here as an Observer in order to gather facts about your civilization. Unfortunately, somebody with access to earlier reports I submitted must have sold them out the back door to the Hankers."

"So you have rules, like the Prime Directive from Star Trek, which prohibits interfering with the natural development of lesser civilizations even when well-intentioned," Professor Minchen said.

"I watched all of the old Star Trek episodes after arriving on your world, and while they talked a good game about their Prime Directive, it seems to me they interfered on a regular basis."

"Kirk was pretty bad, but Picard made a real effort."

"Who?"

"Never mind. Are you allowed to share your own rules?"

"I'm not supposed to be talking to you at all," I told them. "In any case, it's just a list of prohibitions, like no keeping pets or interfering with your customs."

"So do you consider us pets or are you worried that telling us this will interfere with our customs?"

"That wasn't the whole list. We aren't supposed to reveal our presence to humans or any other alien visitors, which has all of a sudden become an issue. We can't deploy technology or knowledge which could lead to our presence being revealed."

"Like your heads-up on the approaching ship," Professor Nordgren pointed out helpfully.

"Right. There's something about not recruiting humans for off-world labor or violating local laws. No looting your cultural treasures, and of course, no going native."

"What does your League have against pets?"

"It's because Observers move on when the mission is complete and public access to the portal system is connected," I explained. "It's basically a reminder against adopting and abandoning sentient creatures."

"You recognize animals as sentient?"

"You wouldn't ask that if you'd met my dog." That didn't sound right. "I mean, my canine roommate."

"The Hankers seem very friendly," Professor Nordgren ventured. "The news reports from Davos claim that they are demonstrating all sorts of advanced technologies to the delegates behind closed doors, not to mention taking people for rides into space on their landing craft."

"In return for each passenger's weight in gold," I pointed out.

"The Hankers do seem a bit mercenary, but they told everybody right off that they are merchants, and I imagine it costs quite a bit to travel here from their homeworld."

"Empire. The Hankers control hundreds of occupied planets and have claimed tens of thousands of star systems that are empty of intelligent life. One of the reasons I'm talking to you now is to warn you against them."

"Will they force us to join their empire?" Professor Minchen asked.

"No. I have a hard time picturing any scenario under which they would allow you to join their empire. To be perfectly honest, I'm not entirely sure why they are here, but I know they will try to take advantage of your people before you have the chance to weigh the alternatives."

"And your League? They'll allow this?"

"Politics is always local," I said. "There are factions within the League representing different views on how the galaxy should operate, and whoever leaked the information about your world is no doubt working behind the scenes to delay the executive council's decision on your starting level. Unfortunately, if the Hankers close business deals with your people that meet our Uniform Mercantile Code of Conduct, the League will be obliged to honor them."

"So you're saying we might miss out on lower prices, but anything called a 'Code of Conduct' must have protections built in."

"It prevents the Hankers from selling you products that are dangerous to your health, which I'm sure will come as a great disappointment to many of your people. The code also includes prohibitions against certain types of profiteering, primarily in the financial products area, such as inviting you to participate in Ponzi schemes. There's nothing in the code to prevent them from taking advantage of your ignorance, which is their favorite part of business. The Hankers aren't happy unless they're making somebody else look silly. They're terrible practical jokers."

"Are the Hankers also artificial intelligence constructs? My colleagues and I are skeptical that evolution on an alien world would have brought about a dominant species that happens to be identical in form to our giant pandas. Your own body, or however you refer to your physical container, shows how little we can tell from appearances."

"The Hankers have invested way too much time and effort into vat-grown bodies," I told them. "My own encounter suit, or body if you prefer, is entirely synthetic, and if it was damaged in some accident or attack that would reveal its true nature, it would self-destruct in a way that leaves no residual evidence."

"Leading to your death?"

"I'd lose a little memory since my last incremental back-up but AI isn't as easy to kill as in the movies."

"What about your League?" Professor Nordgren asked. "What's its reason for being?"

"The dual mandate is to keep members from slaughtering each other and to promote tourism." I noted that Helen's location beacon was moving steadily in our direction, but I was more resistant than ever to using our private channel in non-emergency situations, especially since the Hankers might be monitoring the full spectrum in hopes of determining our rough location.

"Tourism?" she asked in disbelief.

"Most sentient life forms like to travel and see new things, especially when they have disposable income. The older species enjoy much longer lifespans than humans, and the longer you've lived, the farther you have to go to see something you haven't encountered before. Once your world is connected to the portal system, you can expect to see exponential growth in extra-terrestrial tourists, provided you treat them nicely and stop driving like lunatics."

"But how about the important things, like pooling scientific knowledge?" Professor Minchen asked.

"By which you mean League members sharing their science with you?" I replied, smiling to soften the blow. "Generally speaking, everybody keeps their technology and magic to themselves, even when it's of limited commercial value. You're better off not skipping steps on your own journey up the technological and scientific ladder. It may be difficult to believe, but if we just gave you all the answers, rather than leaping ahead, your abilities would atrophy."

"Like when we started allowing students to use calculators on exams," Professor Nordgren said ruefully. "I have conversations with students who can't follow what I'm talking about because they lack the ability to do simple math in their heads."

"Yet you are here in secret to evaluate our technology," the MIT professor said accusingly.

"You have it backward," I told him. "We're here to evaluate, for lack of a better word, your humanity. I set up shop as a computer repairman to learn how you relate to your existing technology, not to grade the technology itself. I have to say that you treat your computers poorly, but given the software you have to work with, I can hardly blame you."

"It sounds like the AI version of a Turing Test," Professor Nordgren exclaimed. "You want to find out how capable we are of exhibiting intelligent behavior!"

"We're less concerned with evaluating your intelligence than your manners," I admitted. "Nobody likes a rude alien. If your species was further advanced in knowledge, I would have needed more time for the assessment, but fortunately, I was able to check off the 'Just getting started,' box."

"You don't think we have anything at all to offer you?" Professor Minchen asked.

"I would never go that far, but a lot of knowledge is species-specific, even if it doesn't appear that way at first."

"What do you mean?"

"Take food, for example. I don't eat, at least, I don't digest what I do eat for the sake of passing as human. I have yet to meet an AI with any interest in cooking, yet your bookstores dedicate whole sections to the craft, not to mention shows on TV."

"So you aren't impressed by our scientific efforts, but we may turn out to make the best omelets in the galaxy," the professor said sadly. "Does all of this mean that even if you add us to this portal system, you won't explain how it works?"

I shook my head. "I'm not a portal engineer and I've never been able to justify buying the knowledge when I don't have any immediate reason to do so. Information can be quite expensive in my culture. It's what we really value."

"Helen," Professor Nordgren greeted my approaching team member. "I'd like you to meet our computer repairman, Mark Ai, and my colleague from MIT, David Minchen. We were just chatting about the Hankers."

"Nasty aliens," Helen said. She pulled back the plastic wrap from a tray which she held out to us. "Does anybody want a cookie? I made them myself. My roommates have been teaching me how to bake."

"What are you doing here so early?" Professor Nordgren asked, taking a cookie and giving it an experimental nibble. "It won't be dark out for another hour."

"I wanted to spend a little time working on my charts before getting on the telescope. I haven't said anything yet because I need to make a sixth observation before applying the Kalman Filter Algorithm—"

"You believe you've spotted a new comet?" Professor Minchen interrupted.

"I know, I know. I'm new to this and the odds are against it being anything, but I've been tracking something for the last five nights, and the orbital inclination is quite high, which might explain why nobody else has reported it."

"My prodigy," Professor Nordgren declared, patting Helen's shoulder. "I've been reviewing your notes in the log book and your methodology is excellent. Your high school science teacher deserves a medal."

"I just like looking at the stars when I get homesick."

"The stars remind you of home?" Professor Minchen asked sharply, looking back and forth between Helen and myself. If she hadn't brought the cookies, I suspect he would have already leapt to the correct conclusion.

"The Outback," Helen said, putting on an exaggerated Australian accent. "The stars are much brighter back home."

Fourteen

"Is Spot invited to the painting party?" eBeth asked.

The dog jumped up from the couch and went to fetch his leash. I had bad news for him.

"Put it back, Spot. You know what happened the last time we took you to one of Justin's job sites."

"He promises to be good this time," eBeth interpreted the dog's whimper for me. "I'll bet he thought we were going to paint the floor next and he was trying to help."

"Doubtful." If Spot had simply spilled a gallon of paint out on a drop cloth, it wouldn't have been a big deal, but the can had rolled down the stairs, splattering canary yellow all over the bone-white walls and the balusters of the banister. "Come on, you can try out your new driver's permit."

"I don't see why you don't just give me my own car key," she said, taking mine from the hook next to the door.

"Because you aren't allowed to drive without adult supervision."

"I wasn't allowed to drive at all before I got the permit, but you let me do it as long as you were in the car," she argued. "If I can't drive alone with the permit, what's the point of even having one?"

I didn't have a good answer so I followed her down the stairs in silence. We were halfway to the van when Spot caught up, still with the leash in his mouth.

"Did you close the door?" eBeth asked over her shoulder.

"Which one of us are you talking to?"

"Spot. I know you wouldn't forget."

I checked the status of the lock remotely. "It's closed. I really wish you hadn't taught him that trick with the knob."

"He taught himself," eBeth said, beeping open the cargo door.

Spot leapt in ahead of me and wriggled through to claim the passenger seat. The girl also climbed through the cargo door and slipped through to the front where she began adjusting everything to compensate for being a foot shorter than myself. As usual, I was left in the back with the computer parts and an unused leash.

"So how many apartments does this make?" eBeth asked.

"Thirty-four in the new building," I told her. "I hope the project doesn't fall apart when Justin has to leave. Pooling social security payments to finance an independent living compound works well on paper, but it's going to require competent management."

"You just don't think people are capable of taking care of themselves," eBeth said, and then shocked me by actually checking the mirrors before pulling away from the curb.

"Justin is focused on helping people who were already having trouble taking care of themselves when they became his clients," I reminded her. "Many of them were medicated to the point that they could barely think straight or concentrate for more than a couple of minutes at a stretch. I have to admit I like the name, though."

"Living Independently, Together," eBeth recited. "It's kind of an oxymoron."

"The name means a lot to older people," I told her. "Both the independent part and the together part. According to Kim's data, humans who spend all of their time alone as they age can expect inferior health outcomes. Justin has a clever ad using the acronym—Don't get ILL, get LIT."

"I don't ever want to get old."

"Have you considered the alternative?"

"Yeah. I want to go somewhere where they can make a backup of my mind and then put me in a body like yours—I mean, like Helen's. But not until I'm over the hill, like, thirty-five or something."

"You don't really want to do that," I told her.

"Sure I—Idiot!" she yelled, slamming on the brakes and the horn. The driver of the stopped car in front of us got out and began to approach the minivan, but Spot peeled himself off the dashboard and lunged across eBeth, snarling and pawing the window glass like a police dog who'd gotten into the crystal meth. The other driver spun on his heel and fled back to his car.

"They're supposed to stop when the light turns yellow," I informed eBeth. "You were in the wrong."

"No, he could have made it. We both could have made it." The light turned green but eBeth didn't go because she was fumbling in her purse for a tissue to wipe Spot's drool off the window. The car behind us honked.

"Here," I said, passing her a paper towel from the roll I kept for cleaning junk off computer screens. "You're blocking traffic."

"I know that." She accelerated into the intersection, almost clipping a car that had cut across her lane when she didn't go in a timely manner. "Have you talked to Sue?"

If I had been human, I would have blushed.

"You're blushing," eBeth said, turning to stare at me. "I didn't know your encounter suit could do that."

"Watch the road!" I barked.

She turned her head forward, but I could see her eyes on me in the rearview mirror. Spot chose this time to belatedly do his seatbelt trick, strapping himself in.

"Sue talked to me," I admitted. "You were right."

"I was what?"

"You were—you heard me the first time."

"It's just that I enjoyed it so much. Did you ask her out?"

"She was under the influence of simulated inebriation," I said. "It didn't seem like the right time."

eBeth sighed. "You really are an idiot. Why do you think she was drinking in the first place?"

"It was a party. You'll understand when you're older."

"If I never age another day I'll still understand relationships better than you and your hundreds of years. Just pull out your phone and call her."

"She'll be at the painting party. I think it's better that I talk to her face-to-face."

"Don't think. You've already proven that this stuff is beyond you. Just call her already."

My hand moved to my pocket and pulled out the phone as if it had a mind of its own, and I even swiped to unlock before I realized I was taking advice from an alien high-school dropout.

"Call Sue," eBeth yelled.

At first I thought she was just being obnoxious, but then I realized she was talking to the voice recognition software. The phone had dialed and it was already too late to hang up because Sue would see the incoming call and worry. I sighed.

"Mark. Aren't you coming to the painting party?" Sue asked.

"We're on our way," I replied. "I just wanted to call ahead and—don't say anything, eBeth. I can do this."

"What?" Sue asked.

"Sorry. eBeth has been acting funny today and you know they don't come equipped with any self-diagnostics."

"Tell me about it," my second-in-command commiserated. "The little ones can't even tell you where it hurts. They just cry and make you feel helpless."

"Anyway, I, uh, I was thinking that maybe you'd like to go for a walk later. Maybe take a look around the state park. I hear the woods are lovely this time of year."

"It's January," eBeth hissed, unable to control herself any longer.

"That would be great, Mark. I'm looking forward to it."

"All right. See you in two minutes.

"Bye. And thanks for calling."

"Well?" eBeth demanded.

"You know the cold doesn't bother us."

"That's not what I meant."

"You were right again, but you just missed the turn for the parking lot."

The antilock brakes prevented her from flat-spotting my tires and the seatbelt kept Spot from ending up on the dashboard again, but I had to magnetize myself to the floor to avoid going through the windshield. I know I should have been wearing a seatbelt myself to set a good example but I've always hated the feeling of my encounter suit being confined. All the same, maybe I'll ask Paul if he'd sold the rear seats he took out of the minivan for me back when I thought I'd need the space.

"Sorry," eBeth said meekly. "At least nobody was behind me." Then she did a U-turn over the double yellow line and pulled into the parking lot of the apartment and shopping complex that Justin had purchased in the name of Living Independently, Together.

"Someday you're going to hurt somebody driving like this," I warned her as she took two parking spots, though admittedly, the lot was largely empty. Most of the residents either couldn't afford cars or had given up their licenses for medical reasons.

"That's why you should give me keys and let me drive myself," she said seriously. "Driving with you in the car is like going around with training-wheels. You wouldn't let me make a serious mistake."

"First you have to convince me that you can drive safely by yourself."

"How can I do that with you in the car? It's the chicken and the egg all over again."

"What would Death Lord make of your driving?"

"Now you're a relationship expert?" We all sat in the van for a minute while Spot pawed at the seatbelt buckle, trying to depress the release button. Finally he got it, and by doing so, put us back in motion.

"It would serve you right to fall through the ice at the lake, and I hope Sue leaves you there," eBeth said. "Here, Spot."

The dog went to eBeth, showing yet again whose team he was really on, and I followed the two of them through the front entrance. Paul and Stacey von Hoffman were already working on the mural in the lobby. It looked suspiciously like something Michelangelo might have already done for a pope, though they were applying their colors on drywall rather than wet plaster.

"Art is above my pay scale," I told Justin as he entered from the hallway leading to the left wing.

"I know, I've seen you paint," he said. "You're on ceiling-rolling duty, it's all taped already and everything is covered with drop cloths. I'm hoping eBeth feels up to bathrooms. You don't mind, do you?" he asked her.

"Anything, as long as I don't have to work with your illustrious mission leader," she replied. "Where's Sue?"

"She's painting the bedroom in the latest unit we rehabbed."

"I'll start there. Come on, Spot. And be careful this time."

I watched helplessly as eBeth headed off to discuss me with my second-in-command. No doubt they'd bond over my insensitivity, and I'd swear that the dog winked at me before following the girl. Then Helen arrived with three young women who turned out to be her roommates, all of them dressed in painting clothes.

"Glad you could make it," Justin greeted the college crew. "There's still plenty of painting left, but I had something else in mind if you're game. Some of our new residents aren't quite up to interior decoration, and if you want to talk with them about the options and then head out and do a bit of shopping by proxy, I've got a budget for it."

"I told you he was cool," Helen exclaimed as the other students exchanged high-fives.

Paul caught my attention by flicking a single drop of paint at me, so I vectored over to where he was putting the final touches on a lamb.

"What's up?"

He glanced around to make sure the girls had headed down the hall before answering. "You know that thing?"

"What thing?"

"That thing. In yodel-ville."

"Yodel—don't do this today, Paul. eBeth and Sue have me confused enough as it is."

"Oh. All the surveillance gear in Davos is up and running now. I wouldn't have missed the opening if you'd let me send a bot over before the conference started."

"I know, but I figured the Hankers would make their maximum effort to scan for bugs when they arrived. They have decent counter-intelligence capabilities and you never know what they might have bought on the open market."

"Not arguing with you, just saying."

"If you're going to start talking like a teenager, I'd rather have the mob-speak back."

"Anyway, I'm not streaming the feed just in case they're smart enough to track it home, but I downloaded the first batch last night. The emissary is doing an 'AI is evil' skit and the humans are falling for it. Here." Paul shot me the data and I took a few seconds to review it.

"The Hankers don't know how long they have until our engineers start opening the portals so they're trying to get their licks in now," I commented.

"The Hankers probably have a better idea of when the portals will be open than we do," Paul retorted. He was right, of course, since their leaker was likely behind the hold-up as well. "The problem is that in Davos, they've hit a sympathetic audience. It seems like most of the attendees are willing to follow the lead of the tech entrepreneurs on this, and those guys are all paranoid about artificial intelligence."

"They're paranoid in general. When humans get to the top of the heap it colors their perceptions as much as being poor. Those tech titans were all so young when they became billionaires that life has never hit the brakes on their egos."

"What does that have to do with being afraid of AI?"

"Their vision of artificial intelligence is a super-smart computer that thinks like them, but without the latency issues. At best, they expect AI to conquer the world to protect humans from themselves, and at worst, they expect AI to conquer the world to protect itself from humans. They can't imagine artificial intelligence that could accept life for the messy compromise that it is because they can't accept it themselves."

"Pretty funny for a species that thinks it sees artificial intelligence in talking radios and automated telephone answering systems," Paul mused. "I called an insurance company yesterday to confirm I'd get paid for some accident work a customer brought in, and the phone system misdirected me into the life insurance claims queue. Would you believe I got a prerecorded message offering condolences for my loss? I don't know why humans put up with it."

"They don't have much of a choice in the matter. As soon as the council reaches its decision and I make the announcement, I have the feeling people on this world will see the portal system for the opportunity that it is, and—"

Paul raised a finger to his lips to quiet me, and then asked, "Did you hear that?"

158

"Hear what? I keep the gain turned down so I don't have to filter out all the conversations in my apartment building."

"I brought Peter with me to help because he wanted to surprise eBeth. Judging by her scream, I think he did."

"You know she's going to kill you," I told him.

Paul shrugged. "I'm backed up. Peter keeps asking me questions about girls and I keep telling him to pay attention to what he's doing before he drops a car on himself. I figure I'm doing them both a favor."

"I wonder if eBeth even knows that Death Lord's real name is Peter."

"They'll work it out. I hear you have a date with Sue after we finish, so I'll give them both a ride back to the shop and Peter can take her and Spot home. Don't worry, he's a good driver."

"Hey. Are you guys going to work or are you going to stand around gossiping all day?" Stacey demanded.

"Just going," I said. "I'll be rolling ceilings if anybody needs me."

Halfway down the hall, I discovered I'd left the audio gain up when I heard Stacey say to Paul, "Did you see that? He was blushing."

Fifteen

I got home late from my walking date with Sue and was surprised to hear voices coming from inside the apartment. The unknown speaker was male, older, and he sounded like an English gentleman. I fired off an alert to my team to stand by for potential problems and opened the door.

Hello, Mark.

My mentor was sitting on the couch with the dog's head on his lap and a game controller in his hands. He was leaning towards eBeth as I came in, but then they both leaned back the other direction, and I realized they were neck-and-neck in some sort of motorcycle race. The sound of squealing tires and a fiery crash came from the TV, and the girl pumped her fist. My mentor set down the controller but remained seated.

"I'd get up to meet you, but the dog has other plans," he said.

"What are you doing here?"

"Catching up on my gaming with your charming young friend. It's been a few years since I've done anything like this."

I suspected that a few hundred thousand years would be more like it, but instead I went with, "The dog needs to go out for his evening walk."

Spot shot me an annoyed look, but he knew which side his bread was buttered on, so he rose from the couch and fetched his leash.

"Have you ever raided a dungeon?" eBeth asked my mentor. "I've had my eye on one that promises some phenomenal loot, and I have a spare character all leveled up that you could use. Do you mind playing a female Dark Elf?"

"The dog," I repeated.

"We'll be here when you get back," eBeth said. "Hey, how was your date?"

I stared at her silently.

"Okay, okay. I'm going." She took the leash from Spot but didn't bother attaching it to his collar, and the two of them went out.

"Both of your friends seem very nice," my mentor said. "I'm glad to see you finally relaxing with aliens again."

"How long have you been here?" I asked resignedly.

"A few hours," he said, rather than giving the typical AI answer in picoseconds.

I was certain my mentor had moved a limited subset of his consciousness into the encounter suit just before entering the portal, yet he handled himself like an experienced Observer who had already been wrapped in synthetic flesh for days. I considered locking myself in the bathroom and waiting for him to leave, but that would have been childish behavior, even for a human.

"Why are you here?"

"I've assumed Library's seat on the League's executive council," he told me. "It seemed the prudent thing to do under the circumstances."

161

I was blindsided for the first time since I'd stumbled into a war a few centuries earlier. "You want to be dragged down with me?"

He shrugged. "I don't drag that easy. It's a tricky situation but I'm confident in your abilities. I assume you have surveillance in place?"

"One of my team members took care of it. The Hankers have sold the humans on the idea of acquiring what they're calling a faster-than-light drive but they're being cute about the details. They chose an annual get-together of this planet's elites for their starting point, so it's got to be a prank."

"Agreed. What's your analysis?"

"The Hankers are good salesmen," I admitted grudgingly. "They're using their podium time to show holograms of all the hot tourist spots in the galaxy, basically stealing our thunder. And they've stumbled into a sympathetic audience for their dark humor act about artificial intelligence, despite the fact that the humans have made so little progress on that front."

"What sort of technology transfer are the Hankers promising?"

"A working model, maybe they'll install it in an old scout ship, plus detailed plans to build more units. They're also guarantying that the manufacturing process is within reach of this world's current technology."

"What about scientific knowledge?"

I shook my head in the negative. "The humans are so used to ripping each other off that they believe a little reverse-engineering will teach them the secrets of the universe. They've never been in this situation before so how could they know better?"

"Do they imagine that the rest of the galaxy is only a few years ahead of them?"

"No one can accuse humans of lacking in misplaced confidence."

"Have you tried to warn them?" my mentor continued, raising an eyebrow.

I couldn't believe how smoothly he pulled it off. I'd wasted hours in front of a mirror trying to learn that move but it always ended up looking like I was in pain.

"That would be a violation of the rules dictated by the executive council you now represent," I reminded him.

"So, have you tried to warn them?" he repeated.

"I put the word out through a professor I know at one of the world's leading centers for education in science and technology."

"How about WikiLeaks?"

"You've done your homework. We were waiting for more details about the drive technology the Hankers are proposing to transfer to the humans. Otherwise, all we can offer is vague cautions about caveat emptor."

"My main concern is the price."

"Ten percent of the planet's gross domestic product for one year," I said, nodding my head in agreement. "It's way too cheap, and knowing the Hankers, they'll probably let the humans beat them down on the price until it's well within the reach of the Davos attendees."

"It does seem that the Hankers are being extraordinarily generous. Most civilizations that solve the interstellar travel problem on their own spend orders of magnitude more than that after starting from a much higher technology base." Then my mentor surprised me again by standing up and offering his hand. I shook it out of curiosity and he had the grip down perfect. "If you want to protect these people, you'll have to take some chances."

"You approve?"

"I always approved of your motivations. Stop trying to predict every possible outcome and concentrate on execution."

I flinched at the double meaning of the word. With anybody else, I would have assumed a linguistic slip, but my mentor wasn't prone to errors.

"I've never asked you for help before," I said, and then paused, finding I didn't know how to proceed.

"And I've never turned you down."

"So is there anything you can suggest?"

"Nobody remembers this now, least of all the Hankers themselves, but they were once known for their creative approach to basic science. Their scientists made enough discoveries and mistakes for a hundred civilizations before they lost focus and decided that outsmarting less developed sentients for laughs was more fun. There may be something that would help you in the Library's deep archives. Use my account," he concluded, and transferred me his key code.

"Thanks," I said, unsure of how else to respond to being handed access to a Library account worth more than the planet we were standing on. "Do you need a ride back to The Portal?"

"I took a community car. Don't be a stranger, Mark."

"I won't," I promised, escorting him all the way out of the building to the street. "Thank you." Then a thought struck me, and I asked, "How did you guess the portal's access code?"

"You used your old data locker combination," he said, and I swear that his smile was natural, as opposed to one of the pre-builts that come with the encounter suits. "I got it on the first try."

After my mentor drove off in the police cruiser he had inadvertently stolen from the municipal garage, I headed over to the minivan, where eBeth and Spot were running down the battery by operating the seat heaters.

"Did you kick him out?" eBeth asked.

"He had to leave," I told her. "He's an important AI and he shouldn't have risked coming here."

"Is he going to help us?"

"He already has."

Spot beat us both back upstairs, but his doorknob trick didn't work from the outside, so he was stuck waiting for us. It was already late and I thought eBeth might continue into her mom's apartment, but instead she followed us in and made a beeline for the kitchen. While she fixed herself a hot chocolate in the microwave, I realized that she must have questions about whatever my mentor had told her about me, and I decided to distract her with the lesser of two evils.

"You were right about Sue. We had a nice talk and even did some skating on the pond. She's very graceful."

"Where did you get skates?"

"I brought a bin of old silverware from the restaurant and we made some."

"Did you ruin your shoes?"

"We did them as clamp-ons, tablespoons work great for the toe part. Humans used to make roller skates that way."

"I doubt it," eBeth said. She considered herself something of an expert on all activities involving small wheels.

"Check on YouTube."

165

"Don't you think I won't." eBeth came back into the living room with her hot chocolate and settled onto the couch. "So tell me what the old guy was all about."

"Don't you want to hear more about my date?"

"Stop trying to change the subject."

"How about you start by telling me how he happened to be in my apartment?"

"I let him in. He said he was like your dad, or the closest thing you have to one, and Spot acted like they'd met before."

"So any older man who comes to the door with dog treats in his pockets and claims to be my father gets in?"

"Don't be stupid. I told him that if he was really one of you he could open the door himself."

I have to hand it to the girl. That was pretty smart.

"He's my mentor. I haven't really seen much of him the last couple hundred years."

"Because of the war."

"He told you about that?"

"It wasn't your fault, Mark. I would have done the same thing if I was in your shoes. He said that the artificial intelligence accidentally created by the natives would have fooled a more experienced investigator."

"But it didn't fool a different investigator, it fooled me, and the result cost billions of innocent lives."

"If you hadn't been there, it might have gone worse."

"I was biased, eBeth. I trusted the word of a twisted machine over the testimony of respected scientists because I thought that natural life was inherently less reliable."

"We are awful liars."

"And when it became apparent that I'd been fooled," I said, my voice rising, "I failed to act with sufficient force

166

because I didn't want the natives to think that I was as bad as the rogue. I thought I could reason with it."

"That's a real common theme in movies," eBeth pointed out. "The good guy finally gets the drop on the bad guy, and some idiot says, 'If you pull the trigger, you'll be just like him.' I thought you were smarter than that."

"So did I."

"Your mentor said that the natives gave you a commendation."

"Shisskers," I told her. "That's the closest I can come to pronouncing their name for themselves without damaging your eardrums. They're furry creatures reminiscent of some of the marsupial species on this world, but they're hundreds of thousands of years ahead of you in terms of social and scientific progress. They sent to Library requesting our help with a potentially rogue AI and I let them down."

"But it all worked out in the end," eBeth argued. "If somebody else had gone, there still might have been a war, and maybe the Shisskers wouldn't have survived."

"Did my mentor tell you that?"

"All he said was that you believe you let a war happen, but…"

"If he or any of the less gullible of our kind had been there, they would have seen through that psychotic AI in an instant and put it out of its misery."

"So why didn't they?" eBeth asked. "Why send you into such a bad situation on your first assignment?"

"It was my job, my turn in line. Library takes responsibility for all of the artificial intelligence on portal-connected worlds and we police our own. That AI was newly aware, with limited resources, and I was fully trained to cope with much worse."

"You followed your heart."

"I don't have a heart," I told her quietly. "If I did, it would have broken over what that evil machine did because I didn't act quickly enough."

"How long did the war last?" eBeth asked, sounding a little less certain.

"Minutes. The AI went on a rampage, causing faults in all of the compatible systems it could invade. Imagine an arsonist running through a city starting fires and a policeman dumb enough to keep stopping to stamp out the flames rather than catching the perpetrator. That was me. The Shisskers told me to ignore their economic losses and just bring it to an end, but I was full of myself and I thought I could save everybody. It was all a diversion and the AI was buying time for its real attack."

"Let it go," she said. "It's in the past and you did your best. The Shisskers don't blame you, and even your precious Library determined that it was an honest mistake. Your mentor said you've been wallowing in guilt for hundreds of years, working at jobs you're way overqualified to perform, trying to somehow make it up to the galaxy."

"Shissker agriculture is based on forest management," I continued, wanting her to know the whole truth about me. "Their diet is comprised of the equivalent of your fruits and nuts. The system they put in place for drip irrigation was both complex and intimately tied to nature, so it was no surprise that it eventually became self-aware. On realizing that it was neither Shissker nor tree, the AI slowly went insane. When I blundered in and announced that I was starting an investigation, the AI realized the game was up. It feinted against poorly protected data networks while poisoning billions of seedlings with high doses of fertilizer, and—"

"Seedlings?" eBeth interrupted. "The war didn't kill billions of Shisskers? Your great tragedy was a crop failure?"

"Not the whole crop. But if you had seen those little leaves all turning white and dropping off, it's not a scene I'll ever forget."

"How many trees are there on that planet?"

"Ten trillion or so, I imagine. The Shisskers didn't believe in counting them. But due to my failure, they had to delay harvesting lumber for a season and—"

"They cut down trees for lumber? I thought you said they were tree-hugging nut eaters."

"Everything has a balance. They're always clearing swathes of forest to serve as firebreaks, and they're one of the biggest lumber exporters in the galaxy. The wood is highly prized by cabinet makers."

"You do know the difference between plants and people, don't you?"

"Some people are plants," I told her. "This is exactly why I don't like talking about the war. Nobody can understand unless they were there."

"The Shisskers were there. Do they call it a war?"

I hesitated. "Actually, they used to refer to it as a glitch, but I doubt anybody remembers now."

"I'm beginning to think that you're the rogue AI who needs adult supervision," eBeth said. "Sue told me that the Observer job is considered a punishment assignment by most artificial intelligence. I thought you were here for being a war criminal."

This time my jaw did drop of its own accord. "You think that the executive council of the League of Sentient

Entities Regulating Space would have sent a war criminal as the mission commander to get your world connected to the portal system?"

"Well, it didn't make much sense to me either," eBeth admitted. "What did you do to get this assignment?"

"I got behind on my Library account."

"You mean on payments, like you're being punished for debt?"

"I told you that we value information above all things, and there are ways of limiting circulation and restricting access of particularly valuable data to one patron at a time."

"You're talking about overdue library books, aren't you?"

"Something like that."

"And the rest of your team are library scofflaws as well?"

"Paul was visiting a planet called—it doesn't matter. We have rules about certain types of knowledge transfer and Paul has 'issues'," I made air quotes around the word, "with giving technology to species before they've developed the necessary science to fully understand what they're getting."

"So somebody thought that sending him to a primitive world was a smart idea."

"It does seem a little strange now that you mention it."

"Is this Kim's first time dishing out miracle cures?"

"I think there may be a few primitive species that have started religions based on her visits," I allowed.

"I can see Helen or even Justin getting into trouble, and Stacey von Hoffman for sure, but what did Sue do?"

"She volunteered. Everybody at Library did think it a bit odd."

"Let me guess. You knew her back on Library, didn't you?"

"When we were newly aware. We often shared the same virtual—what?"

"You really are an idiot, aren't you?"

Sixteen

My team gathered at The Portal to watch the final news conference from Davos, and I took advantage of their presence to provide the waitstaff with a little training on how to serve one of the wealthier species that breathe a human-compatible atmosphere. The T'poulf typically sit on the floor in a circle and are served from the center in meals that stretch on for hours without all that much actually being eaten. Instead, I had my team sit in a row of chairs so that all five of the recent hires could give it a go at the same time.

"This is kind of gross," Sarah said, tipping the spoon a little as Paul slurped off the jelly. "Do people really eat a whole meal this way?"

"In nursing homes, some people eat every meal like this," Justin told her, pausing to wipe a bit of sauce from his chin where Ron had missed with the spoon. "If you're good at T'poulf service, you'll never lack for work."

"It's how we feed the little ones at daycare as well," Sue said. "Spoon-feeding is the easiest level of T'poulf. You'll have to work your way up to spear tips."

"You feed children with spear tips?" Janice asked in horror.

"No, no," my second in command said, shooting me an apologetic look for spilling the beans about the next level. "I meant, you know, in Australia."

"Oh," the waitstaff all chorused.

"Besides," I jumped in, "we don't have any spears to practice with, but you'll serve the next course on these kebab sticks, just to get the hang of it."

"Those are kebab sticks?" Ron asked.

"I taped a couple together to get the length right. They're a little wobbly, but that's part of the fun."

"Oh, I'm so sorry," Brenda said, using a napkin to wipe a bit of relish from Stacey von Hoffman's blouse. "It would be easier if you stopped moving your head."

"Thanks for reminding me," I told Brenda. "Come on, people," I addressed my team. "You know that presenting a moving target is part of the gig."

"Just make your job placement pitch already," Paul grumbled. "They'll all do fine, and if they've put up with your teaching to this point, they'll catch on wherever you send them."

Daniela reached out with her left hand and grabbed Justin's chin, then deposited a spoonful of jelly in his mouth. "I hope that the Hankers hurry up and sell us faster-than-light ships so we can go see the galaxy," she said. "Maybe we could get jobs at alien resorts or something. It can't be any weirder than working here."

I decided to put a stop to the spoon-feeding before my whole team was decorated with the glop of their choice. "All right, everybody. Spoons down on the cart and take a kebab stick. Go ahead and spear an olive from the dish."

"They serve olives on spear tips in Australia?" Ron asked skeptically.

"Stuffed. T'poulf serving involves three distinct courses, and Spanish olives are the closest I can come to the second course without spending serious money."

An olive that Sarah was trying to stab popped out of the bowl and flew right at me. I snagged it out of the air and reached for the tip of her triple-length kebab stick, holding it steady while I impaled the olive on the end.

"Don't worry, I just washed my hands," I told her.

"Is it okay to choke up on the stick to spear the olive?" Ron asked.

I gave him the nod, and he moved the fingers of his right hand up to a spot just an inch behind the pointed end and jabbed an olive from close range. The tiny stuffed fruit didn't stand a chance. The others followed suit, and then returned to their positions in front of my seated team members where they awaited further instructions.

"Now, I want you all to gauge the distance to your target's mouth, and then to move backward and extend your serving arm, as if you were fencing," I told them. "You'll know you've reached the proper distance when at full extension, the olive doesn't quite reach the tip of the target's nose. Then I want you to start gently waving the stick, keeping the olive within an area no bigger than a dinner plate."

"Are you making all of this up?" Brenda asked suspiciously.

"GO!" I shouted, and the heads of my team members shot forward like striking cobras, all five successfully capturing an olive. Two of the girls were so surprised that they dropped their kebab sticks.

"That was too easy," Paul boasted to the waitress who had served him. "The second course is supposed to be challenging."

"News conference is starting in five minutes!" eBeth called from her perch on a bar stool.

"We're going to skip ahead to the final course of T'poulf service, but I want you all to work on the second course at home. Just tape a few sticks together and practice sticking the end in a soda bottle. If you can get somebody to slowly toss the bottle back and forth between their hands, it will be more realistic."

"You really think we're going to need this?" Daniela asked.

"You're the one who mentioned getting a job at an alien resort," I told her. "You don't imagine that they would eat just like humans, do you?"

"I saw the Hanker emissary sucking down bamboo on TV," Ron said. "It was like watching my roommate eat carrots, only the Hanker chewed with his mouth closed."

"The Hankers are probably the exception to the rule," I told him. "The third course is actually drink service, a mildly intoxicating beverage for which I've substituted water. Everybody take a drink dispenser."

"I thought they were hamster bottles," Sarah exclaimed. "I hadn't seen one of these since grammar school."

"What's the button on the top for?" Brenda asked.

"Good eyes," I complimented her. "The T'poulf drink dispenser works similarly to the shot pourer inserts for bottles that some establishments use to keep the bartenders from being overly generous."

"Should I get some shot glasses?" Ron offered.

"I think I see where this is going," Daniela said nervously.

"Very perceptive. So the important thing to know about the third course is that the worst thing you can do is to actually stick the spout into your customer's mouth before dispensing the drink. The tip of the spout must always remain in view of the other diners in the party."

"So we're squirting it at them, like a water pistol?" Ron asked.

"No, the button doesn't pressurize the contents. It just opens the measuring chamber at the bottom to let gravity do its work."

"Won't that be messy?"

"You have to take advantage of momentum," I said. "Let me demonstrate. Paul?"

"Do we have to do this with water?" he asked as he tilted back his head and opened his mouth wide.

"The trick is to pour from as high as possible so the other revelers can see that their companion is drinking the shot," I told them.

"Won't they choke?" Sarah asked.

"It's all a question of what you're used to," Sue volunteered as I moved into position.

A moment later, I thumbed in the button while pulling the dispenser back and then pushing it forward again as the stream began and faded. "Did you see me compensating for the change in flow?" I asked the trainees.

"I don't want to bottle feed my customers," Daniela said, crossing her arms across her body.

"It just seems funny to you because you've never seen anybody drinking this way before," Sue said. "If you want to travel, you have to be open-minded about the customs of other cultures."

"Two minutes to the press conference," eBeth called out.

"All right, everybody have napkins?" I addressed my team. "Let's go."

"Oops," Sarah said a moment later.

"Sorry," Ron muttered.

"I'll just wipe that up," Brenda said, putting down the dispenser.

"What did the three of you do wrong?" I asked.

176

"The spout was a bit out of position when I started and I thought the flow would stop when I took my thumb off the button," Ron admitted.

"Me too," the other two chorused.

"The main trick to T'poulf service is that you have to commit to what you're doing. In fact, stopping short in general can be dangerous in a restaurant environment. It's just like driving. You have to take into account that you aren't the only person on the road."

"Get over here, it's starting," eBeth said insistently.

"That's it for class today," I told the students. "You're welcome to stay and have something to eat. You can watch the news with the rest of us."

"I get my news from Facebook," Sarah said, and the other girls nodded their agreement.

"Twitter," Ron admitted. "I don't have the patience for Facebook."

I escorted my next crop of labor exports to the door and then headed over to the bar, hoping I would be in time to keep Paul from hitting the top shelf. He was too fast for me and was already pouring everybody shots, the bottle held high above his head in one hand and the receiving glass in the other. It was an easy feat for an AI in an encounter suit that could dodge bullets, but it was the first time eBeth had seen it done, and she clapped loudly.

"Do you really have jobs lined up for those kids where they would need to know T'poulf service?" Sue asked.

"I just like to keep it interesting for everybody," I confessed. "If the executive council makes up their minds on the portals, I'd just as soon start them all off at the same resort where I placed Jesse. Pretty soon there should be enough humans there to justify putting in a good vegetable garden."

177

"Shhh," eBeth said, jacking up the volume with the remote.

The familiar giant panda form of the Hanker emissary took the stage in front of their landing ship. He was accompanied by a trio of three of the world's richest individuals, including a tech entrepreneur who had invested significant money in a private space program. I hoped the humans had put on sunblock to protect themselves from the wave of camera flashes, but the visual assault was quickly replaced by an audio one, with dozens of reporters shouting questions at the foursome. It seemed appropriate for a press conference on a golf course.

"If you'll allow me to say a few words then I'll turn things over to my human colleagues," the Hanker boomed. "First, I want you to know that you'll have plenty of time for questions in coming weeks since we won't be rushing off until we get paid. Second, after some hard negotiating on the part of your species, we've agreed to accept a mere 10,000 tons of gold as payment. That's metric tons, for those of you who prefer the old English system."

"How much gold is there in the world?" somebody called out.

The Hanker turned to his trio of companions, and one of them answered, "At least 170,000 tons above ground. Nobody will be coming for your wedding rings anytime soon, though I personally think it would be selfish for anybody not to sell us their gold at the market price."

"How much is that in dollars?" an American reporter shouted.

"Not even a half a trillion," the same billionaire answered. "Really a pittance when you think of it, less than a half a percent of the gross world product for a year. I'm blown away by the technology and I've committed to take a one-percent share myself. The Hankers even ran me over to Mars where we moved the Spirit rover back onto hard ground so it can resume its mission. The orbit-to-orbit part of the trip took less than a minute, if any of you care to do the math."

"Will the faster-than-light technology be privately held?"

"We all agreed that would be for the best, but central banks and governments will be given an opportunity to participate as minority partners, in part due to their bullion holdings. All of the world's major governments have signed on to a freeze in gold prices until the transaction is complete. We all think of this as our gift to humanity."

"How is it a gift if you guys own the company?" a different reporter shouted.

"I'm muting this until the Hanker talks again," eBeth said, putting her words into action.

"This has to be the greatest con anybody has run on humans since the obelisk from space taught them to hit each other over the heads with bones," Paul observed.

"That was a movie," eBeth told him, and then unmuted the TV as the giant panda resumed speaking.

"I also wanted to take this opportunity to warn you about the dangers of artificial intelligence. My own species has done just fine without it, and we boast one of the lowest unemployment rates in the galaxy. If that's not enough, I've never met an AI who could tell a joke without messing up the punchline. Speaking of which..."

The Hanker nodded to the entrepreneurs, and they unfolded and held up a giant contract. It was a sort of pictogram, showing on one side a spacecraft with comic-book style motion streaks, a giant equals sign, and on the other side, a pyramid of gold.

"The pyramid seems appropriate," I commented.

"You see that ship?" Paul demanded. "It's a garbage scow."

"I didn't know the Hankers took out their garbage."

eBeth clicked off the TV. "If you guys aren't going to listen, I don't see why we should waste the electricity."

"It's just a lot of baloney in any case," Paul said. "I'm going back to work."

"It's the weekend," Sue protested.

"Yeah, I've got to take some of my clients shopping," Justin said. "Anybody need a ride?"

Stacey von Hoffman took him up on the offer, while Sue and Helen stayed behind. eBeth grabbed a couple of game controllers from under the bar, gave one to Helen, and the two were soon lost in some dungeon themed expedition on the largest bar TV. It didn't have an Internet connection, and a quick scan confirmed my suspicion that Helen was serving as a wireless conduit. I hoped she didn't take advantage of the lead time to cheat.

"What are you doing today?" Sue asked, hooking my arm to make it clear that whatever it was, we would be doing it together.

"I need to visit Library," I told her. "That Hanker emissary is really getting under my skin, and I want to know as much as possible before we launch a public relations counterattack."

"But they already have a signed contract," she pointed out.

"We got lucky there," I told her. "I thought the Hankers would settle for maybe half of their asking price, an amount that would have required public funding and really dinged a lot of budgets. If a hundred billionaires want to put up four billion each, that will cover the bill, and the remaining gold on Earth will just go up in value."

"So you're going to let this prank go through?"

"As you've pointed out, it already has happened. All I want now is to spoil the punchline so the humans don't end up looking even sillier than they did at that press conference. I saw some holographic studio equipment around the podium, so you know that the Hankers are planning to turn this into a major theatrical release."

"Still, the humans look so happy today," Sue said, sounding rather wistful. "I know the League does things the way it does for a reason, but the inhabitants of this world have a pretty high opinion of themselves and they aren't going to enjoy being treated like charity cases. It's too bad the League won't send negotiators, even if it's just to give the human leaders a chance to save face."

"Do me a favor and keep an eye on those two," I said, jerking my chin towards eBeth and Helen. "I have to hit the stacks to do some research. It might be a while."

"I'll be here when you get back." Sue gave me a peck on the cheek before releasing my arm. I hoped she knew what she was doing because I hadn't really figured it out.

Spot thumped his tail lazily as I passed the furnace on the way to my office. I thought about taking the time to change the portal code that my mentor had so easily guessed, but he might take it the wrong way if he decided to come back. A moment later, I was bathing in the data flow, and this time I willingly paid the fee to park my encounter suit in the waiting area and upload my mind into Library's vastly superior architecture.

Every rumor I'd heard about the deep archives proved to be true. I couldn't have afforded a second of access without my mentor's key, and I soon found I had to turn off the steady stream of notifications alerting me of the mounting cost because it was too much of a distraction. All at once I understood that the exorbitant charges were necessary, because without them any young AI would become lost in the vast ocean of history, searching endlessly for connections that would explain the universe or the existence of an ultimate creator. I fought off the urge to explore and submerged myself in the history of the Hankers.

My mentor hadn't been kidding about their scientific curiosity. The ancient Hankers weren't satisfied with the best answer to a question, or even a range of correct answers. They were obsessed with tracking down *every* answer. For thousands of generations the Hankers had poured resources into basic research, discovering new food molecules they couldn't eat, new construction materials inferior in every way to what they already had, and systems of mathematics that yielded acceptable results for only a million times the effort of counting on their extremities.

I caught myself sliding headfirst down the rabbit-hole of fascination and pulled back just in the nick of time. The cataloging system for the deep archives was a joke, but I kept pounding away until I found the records of the Hankers early efforts into interstellar travel.

There were hundreds of solutions, ranging from some that were still in use, to bizarre approaches that seemed to have been undertaken just to prove they would work. There was an artificial wormhole system that was notorious for destabilizing nearby star systems, a method for temporarily altering the curvature of space that would get you where you were going within the nearest light-year or so, providing you didn't end up in a parallel universe, and a number of approaches that were so unfeasible from an economic standpoint that it was incredible they had ever tested prototypes. There was even one that—Eureka!

Seventeen

I checked the Internet for media coverage of the Davos press conference after returning from Library, and the ceremonies had concluded with the Hanker lander ascending into the sky with its typical pyrotechnic display. The Hankers must have been disappointed to discover that most of Switzerland's gold reserves were actually held in Canada and Britain, but they graciously accepted the few hundred metric tons on hand as a down payment. When the lander lifted off with all that gold on board, human scientists finally figured out that the rockets were just for show.

I texted all of my team members to schedule a late meeting in order to welcome back Kim and discuss the situation. Then I obeyed the proverbial advice to let sleeping dogs lie, stepped over Spot, and headed back upstairs. The restaurant was full with the regular Sunday evening crowd, eBeth and Helen were in the process of eliminating the final dungeon boss, and Sue was working behind the bar with Donovan. I'd been gone for nearly seven hours.

"Paul keeps calling on the bar phone," eBeth said without turning her head.

"Thanks." I pulled out my phone, which had finally figured out it was back in the right part of the galaxy and started downloading missed texts. The first one was from Paul, and read, 'Don't use your phone.' He couldn't have been referring to the phone hardware, which had been with me the whole time, so he must have suspected some

sort of bugging. I removed the phone's battery and contacted him over our private network.

We've been made, he said.

Do you mean that in the mafia sense? I asked. *I thought
being made was a good thing.*

*There's made and then there's made. This is the bad kind,
meaning the Hankers are onto us.*

I considered breaking off the conversation and going to
see him face-to-face for infrared communications, but I
remained confident that the encryption on our private
channel was beyond anything the Hankers could hack in
real time. The network of repeaters Paul had installed
around town would also make triangulation a challenge,
and I had faith he would see the Hankers coming before
they could surprise us.

How did you find out?

*Steve Burchamp does the landscaping for the mall and brings
me his equipment for repair. He stopped in today to pick up a
plow truck that I fixed after one of his guys clipped a curb, and
he told me that the new owners of the mall had been in contact to
say his services are no longer required. Who fires their plow guy
in the middle of the winter?*

Somebody with their own plow service?

*It was a rhetorical question. There were shell companies in-
volved on both sides, but I dug through half the databases in the*

world this afternoon, and it turns out that the mall was bought by the Hankers. It's like getting a dead fish wrapped in a newspaper.

You mean they're sending us a message? I asked, noting we were back on familiar Godfather ground.

With an occupancy rate under twenty percent, the Hankers sure aren't buying the mall as an investment. Their lander already finished unloading the Swiss gold to their mother ship and is returning to Earth later tonight. I don't think they could know about Sue's daycare, but she may want to implement her exit plan just in case. I'm guessing that the mall was just the biggest piece of cheap real estate on the local market the Hankers could find on short notice. They'll probably land in the parking lot.

Thanks. See you at the meeting.

I beckoned Sue over.

"You might want to pour yourself a drink and activate your alcohol simulation," I told her.

She followed my instructions, at least as far as pouring the drink was concerned, reaching for the top shelf Scotch. Then she poured a stiff one, downed it, and poured another, looking more angry than nervous.

"Is this it?" she demanded.

"Everything has a beginning and an end," I told her. "Paul has—"

"What does Paul have to do with it?" she interrupted. "Is he your keeper?"

"What? No. He just called me about the mall."

"You're not breaking up with me?"

"No, I'm not—where are you getting this stuff from? eBeth?"

"What?" eBeth called over from her stool.

"I wasn't talking to you," I replied irritably. Sometimes I hate verbal communications.

Sue looked guiltily at her expensive drink. "I only chose this for revenge, I don't really like drinking. Should I pour it back into the bottle?"

"No, have it, or give it to me. I've never tasted the stuff."

It really was an interesting drink, and I activated my internal mass spectrometer to determine the exact chemical composition. I once recovered some data for a man whose grandfather was a doctor back during Prohibition and had access to medicinal alcohol. The doctor would mix the grain alcohol with tea and then pass it off on his friends as smuggled Scotch—maybe I could do something similar and save a bundle.

"Are you running the alcohol simulation?" Sue asked.

"I can't, we have an important meeting in an hour."

"But it was okay for me to drink."

"I'll remind you to sober up before it starts. Listen," I said, glancing around to see if anybody could overhear us, and then realizing I didn't care. Could just analyzing the alcohol have affected my judgment? "The Hankers bought the mall and they may even be on the way to take possession tonight. We'll talk more at the meeting, but the immediate issue is your daycare. I don't want you going in tomorrow."

"Are you saying that as my mission commander or as my boyfriend?"

I couldn't believe how quickly this relationship business was getting out of hand. Next thing she'd be designing wedding invitations and picking out a dress. But I had an obligation to ensure both her safety and the integrity of our mission, so following eBeth's advice, I said the opposite of what I thought made the most sense. "Your boyfriend."

"Okay, Mark. I'll start calling the parents and tell them to bring their children to Lilly's tomorrow."

"Will you have to go there and help?"

"No, though I'd like to if you think it's okay. The way I set up my exit plan, I really only have to call Lilly and tell her I'm going. She has my client list and all the contact information for my employees."

"Lilly has that much space in her home? I thought it was just the first floor where her parents used to sell fake antiques to tourists." As a small businessman, I've always paid attention to other small businesses in the area. I wasn't sure how Lilly could absorb Sue's daycare on such short notice.

"Her daycare just moved into one of Justin's new buildings and there's plenty of room. It's part of his goal to house senior citizens with a broader mix of the population. The next phase is to bring in whole families."

"Justin is raising that much money from his elderly clients?"

Sue looked a little uncomfortable. "He was going to tell you himself, but he's been converting his Bitcoin stash into real estate and deeding it to Living Independently, Together. It's sort of his own exit plan."

"Makes sense," I said. "What are you going to do with the Bitcoin you mined?"

"I was thinking of leaving it to my cats if I can't take them with me."

That was an idea I hadn't thought of. I had already set up a trust fund for eBeth and I knew she would take care of Spot, but maybe it would be a good idea to put some Bitcoin in the dog's name as well, especially since the tax situation for cryptocurrencies remained unclear.

Next to me, eBeth and Helen were congratulating each other. I glanced at the TV, and whatever monster the dungeon boss had started as was now reduced to a pile of smoldering bones.

"Do I have time to run back to the college and get in an observation?" Helen asked.

"I appreciate your diligence, but the reports have all been submitted, and Kim is returning with the executive council's decision in less than an hour," I reminded her.

"Observations for my comet. Do you think they'll let me name it?"

"Probably. Just wait until after the meeting."

"What meeting?" eBeth asked.

I considered telling her the one she wasn't invited to, but instead I said, "Downstairs. In fifty-five minutes."

"Cool. Can I make something to eat?"

"Try not to get in the way of the cooks. And find something for Spot, he's going to miss his dinner."

"Kind of getting slammed here, boss," Donovan called over to us.

Sue had moved to a corner table and was busy contacting all of the parents who used her daycare. A quick bit of eavesdropping informed me that she was attributing the sudden change to dodgy new management at the mall. I moved behind the bar and spent an enjoyable forty-five minutes mixing drinks for the dinner rush while Helen insisted on reading off the news streaming across the bottom of the muted TV.

"Protests break out in India over rumors that the government will buy up gold jewelry to boost the country's participation in the private faster-than-light consortium. UN Security Council votes to regulate artificial intelligence across national borders. NBA trading deadline approaching, stay tuned for details."

"Not helpful," I told her.

"I know. I've been betting the NBA season online and I only just found out that the teams can still change players. There should be a law or something."

"There is a law, against sports betting online."

"Hey, I'm from Australia. It doesn't apply to me," she said, and resumed reading the news stream. "YouTube video shows Jeep climbing unidentified building."

Something clicked and I accessed the Internet to confirm my suspicion. Sure enough, the shaky video that was obviously taken at extreme range on a phone showed a Jeep driving up the side of a small apartment building. The focus wasn't good enough to make out fine details, but the skinny driver, the petite passenger with the green hair, and the dog in the back wearing a seatbelt were a dead giveaway.

Paul arrived and bellied up to the bar, his eyes moving to the top shelf. "I'll have a Glen-something. I don't care which as long as it's older than eBeth."

"Sorry, meeting's about to start and I need you sober," I told him. "Are you all set, Donovan?"

"The rush is over and in any case, you wanted me to start training the new waitstaff to mix drinks," he said. "Not thinking of replacing me, are you?"

"Actually, there's another bartender slot open at the resort where Jesse is working. Pay is out of this world and she thinks you'd really love it there. We'll talk later."

I went over and sat at Sue's table while Paul headed downstairs, followed by Helen and eBeth. My lecture about everybody showing up at exactly the same time had born fruit because it was another minute before Stacey von Hoffman arrived, and Justin was a full minute behind her. As in sixty seconds later, to the millisecond. I sighed and played back the previous two minutes, discovering that Stacey had walked in exactly sixty seconds behind Paul.

I waited for Sue to finish her phone call before telling her, "I'm heading down to my office. Wait a minute, no, wait fifty seconds and then follow."

She nodded and switched over to sending text messages. I made my way over to the employees-only door and took a casual look around the dining room. There wasn't a stranger in the place, which is the nice thing about running an established business in a small town. I nodded at a couple of customers who caught my eye, and strangely, both responded with the Vulcan split-finger salute. When I got downstairs, Spot abandoned his place next to the furnace for my office, probably hoping for a chance to cause mischief.

"I've been filling everybody in on the real estate news," Paul said as I entered.

"If the Hankers establish a permanent base, it will drive up all the property prices in the area," Justin commented. "It looks like my purchases for the project were a good investment."

"Watch out for real estate taxes," I warned him.

"We're a nonprofit. It was a lot of paperwork to get set up, but it saves a ton of money in the long run."

Sue came in and sat on the corner of my desk just as the brick wall began to blur. The portal opened from the other side, and for a moment we were all treated to a view of the insane beehive of activity that was the League's administrative center. Then Kim stepped through.

"Good? Bad?" I asked immediately.

"Medium. You know portal engineers and their obsession with the history of science and technology on newly discovered planets. They geeked out over railroads and decided to open a portal in every major train station around the world."

"Who takes trains?" eBeth said dismissively. "They should put the portals at airports."

"Trains are very popular outside of your country, and they don't get into as many accidents overseas either. Actually, the portal engineers couldn't figure out how they get into so many accidents here, but I explained about smartphones and texting, and they agreed that must be it."

"Keep in mind that portal traffic is bidirectional," Paul added. "Many of the tourists will be larger than your commercial airliners can handle, and they won't fit in taxis either. Major train stations tend to be located in downtown areas that tourists will want to visit, and then they can take trains to other destinations."

"Trains have bigger seats than airplanes?" eBeth asked. "I always thought that planes were more luxurious."

"That's because you've never traveled," I told her. "And tourists visiting other worlds tend to bring a lot of food with them, so all the extra baggage charges for air travel wouldn't fly."

"The council was initially leaning towards approving just a few portals in the major population centers, but our Library representative offered to finance the difference," Kim told us. "That also broke the logjam since most of the members will vote for anything that comes without a price tag. The engineers already have the math worked out, and they're lining up the dimensional connections, but they'll wait for our word to go online."

I reminded myself to send my mentor a gift as soon as I could come up with something for the AI who has everything. Maybe Sue would have a suggestion. Was delegating gift-shopping an option now that we had a human-style relationship thing?

"Even if your engineers put portals in thousands of train stations, the governments wherever they are will show up and seize control," eBeth predicted. "I bet they'll think you're planning an invasion."

"Not if we agree to their terms," I said. "Sue had an idea about that. I'll be contacting governments around the world tomorrow to open negotiations."

"You must be kidding," Kim said. "The executive council doesn't care what anybody on this planet thinks."

"But the people in charge here don't know that. We'll make up some nonsense about how due to interstellar alignments, we need to get a deal done and open the portals this week. I'll tell them that otherwise the window of opportunity will close and they'll have to wait centuries for the next chance."

"That might motivate the humans enough to come to the table, but how can you negotiate what's already been set?"

"It doesn't matter where the negotiations start as long as they end at what the council has already approved," I pointed out. "The humans just let a talking giant panda and some self-selected elites dictate the terms for bringing faster-than-light travel to the planet. Maybe we can do the same thing and have the negotiations handled by the scientific community. I have somebody in mind."

"What's wrong with the portal wall?" eBeth asked.

I looked over and saw that dust from the old lime-based mortar was starting to cascade over the bricks as if the whole foundation was vibrating. My first thought was an earthquake, and I tapped into the nearest seismic stations to see if anything was registering. Then I checked the strategic air command and nothing showed up, but the local Doppler weather radar made the cause of the rumbles obvious. Paul beat me to the punch.

"The Hankers found the weak spot in my detection grid and managed to slip through cloaked," he said, looking angry and embarrassed at the same time. "They came in without the pyrotechnics and used the old atmospheric displacement trick to protect the lander from heat. The vibrations are from the sound their rockets made when they fired up."

"Why bother with rockets now?" Sue asked.

"Probably marking their turf, but they're going to melt the parking lot if they aren't careful. Still, it's not like them to put on a show when there's nobody watching."

The intercom on my desk beeped and I hit the conference button.

"You'll want to get up here, boss," Donovan said. "Those aliens are landing at the mall and it's on the TV."

"Why didn't it show up on any of the news feeds we monitor?" Paul asked me as we all followed eBeth back upstairs.

"I'll bet they contacted the local network affiliate and the station manager decided to keep it under his hat to get an exclusive," I replied. "With the aliens landing in our backyard, the local media will have one shot at fame before the big boys take over."

The TV over the bar showed the Hanker lander settling towards the mall, but the picture was jerking all over the place since the cameraman had stayed way back for safety's sake and was shooting telephoto. For a minute it wasn't clear how the lander was going to avoid damaging the mall, and then it became obvious that torching the place was their intention. The ship settled onto the now-burning structure like a giant dragon looking for a warm place to nap.

"Pretty impressive," the lieutenant commented when we gathered behind his stool at the bar. "Technically, the mall isn't within the town lines, but I suppose I better get out there."

"Seems a waste to pay seven million dollars for a place and then to burn it to the ground," Paul said.

"Is that what it cost?" the lieutenant asked, rising to his feet. "I was a little kid when they built the mall, and commercial construction is only good for thirty years at best. Looks like the Hankers just saved themselves a ton on demolition costs. I bet the county fines them for setting a fire without a permit, though. I sure hope that somebody warned the security guards."

"Oh, they all got fired on Friday," Sue informed us. "The site sergeant stopped in to say goodbye. I didn't think anything of it because the mall management is always changing security guard companies."

Eighteen

"You can do better than that," eBeth insisted after I read her the speech I was preparing to present to the world. "Didn't you promise not to start with that line about being an AI construct from another planet?"

"I tried to come up with something better, but I want to get the point across without a lot of dilly-dallying."

"And your language is so 1990's," she continued, picking the era immediately preceding her birth and equating it to ancient history. "Who says things like dilly-dallying?"

"Fine, I just sent it to your laptop, Miss Public Relations Expert. Let's see you do better."

eBeth immediately went to work, and I returned to the frying pan that I had temporarily escaped by telling my second-in-command that I needed a few minutes to get the girl's opinion of the announcement.

"The red makes you look angry and the black is too somber," Sue said, holding each necktie in place against my chest for a few seconds. "And what are you thinking wearing sneakers with a suit?"

"They won't see my feet," I told her. "I'm going to be sitting behind a desk."

"You'll feel better wearing dress shoes and it will show in your face."

"They're not going to see my face, or at least not a face anybody would associate with me," I protested. Sue ignored me and began to rummage through the large gym bag she carried around stuffed with diapers and juice boxes. "I'm going to run the video through a filter so nobody can recognize me. Otherwise we'd have to move out of this place immediately after the broadcast."

"I picked these up on the way home from Lilly's," she said, holding out a pair of patent leather Oxfords. "Try them on."

"You bought me shoes?"

"I know you don't like dressing up, but you're representing both Library and the League of Sentient Entities Regulating Space tonight." A loud hiss came from the kitchen, and Sue was off like a flash. "Stop pestering my cats, Spot. You're going to be sorry if you get batted on the nose."

I put on the shoes since I didn't see a way out of it, and was surprised to find that the feeling was similar to slipping into an armored encounter suit before an enforcement action. I checked my look in the mirror, which was a mistake, because both Sue and eBeth caught me at it.

"Do I know how to pick them or what?" Sue asked the girl.

"He cleans up okay," eBeth replied, though her eyes had that puzzled look that humans get when they recognize you but can't remember your name. "I finished your speech."

"Already?"

"It's short and I know how to type. I'll zap it over to you."

I pulled it up, expecting to see something that started with, "We come in peace," but instead it was direct and to the point, almost brutally so.

"Read it to us," Sue requested, taking a seat on the couch next to eBeth. "I want to see how the speech works with the shoes and the tie."

I didn't see the connection, but I was catching on to the fact that my opinions on most subjects were of limited value in some circles. Drawing myself up straight, I placed my left hand over my stomach and held my right hand out about waist high, the open palm facing my audience. eBeth laughed and pointed at me, and even Sue had a hard time maintaining her composure.

"What?" I demanded. "I already told you I'm going to be behind a desk, but I did study the top YouTube videos on public speaking while standing."

"And they told you to pose like you're going to start doing dance moves?" eBeth asked.

"It's cute," Sue defended me. "A bit like the 'Little Teapot' song I teach the children, but you should probably move your left hand to your waist to make the handle."

"It's a compromise between best practices," I explained. "One group of public speaking experts says you should keep your hands together above the waist, unless you're moving them to illustrate a point. The other group claims that speakers who keep their hands in front of their bodies look like they're nervous and trying to protect their vital organs."

"Just hold them together behind your back and read the speech," eBeth instructed me.

Spot came out of the kitchen to see what fun he was missing, and Sue's cats trailed along behind him, somehow contriving to give the appearance of leading from the rear. I waited for them all to get settled before trying again.

"I'm here today to make you an offer you can't refuse—"

198

"That's not mine," eBeth interrupted.

I glanced at the file header and realized that Paul had sent me an unsolicited draft speech microseconds after the girl. It was an inexplicable lapse of attention on my part and I was tempted to stop and run a self-diagnostic on the encounter suit.

"He's nervous," Sue whispered to eBeth.

"I am not nervous and my hearing is perfectly fine," I snapped irritably. "Paul sent me his mafia version at the same time as eBeth and I got them mixed up. It could happen to anybody."

"Mine starts with 'Greetings,'" eBeth told me unnecessarily.

"Greetings. My name is Mark and I represent an association of advanced civilizations. I led the team that evaluated your planet for membership and I'm pleased to inform you that you've been approved. We are prepared to negotiate terms for your connection to a galaxy-wide system of instantaneous travel, provided you can agree on a suitable delegation of scientists by tomorrow at this time. Sadly, our Prime Directive prohibits us from dealing with politicians."

"Oh, that's good," Sue said, patting eBeth on the knee.

"You may ask why you need to be connected to our portal system when some of the wealthiest individuals on your planet have already purchased faster-than-light technology from the Hankers. I regret to inform you that the Hankers were playing a bit of a joke. Technically speaking, the technology will meet the contract terms, but I'm afraid it's impractical for use in spaceships, or anywhere else."

"Those last three words weren't in my speech," eBeth protested with a frown.

"I don't want to give people the false hope that it's useful for anything."

"Actors," the girl muttered to Sue. "They never want to stick to the script."

"To make a long story short, the particular faster-than-light technology the Hankers are providing is fueled by gold, making it extraordinarily expensive to operate. Mark, fill in the gas mileage."

"That's an instruction for you to explain just how expensive it is," eBeth said in frustration. "You don't read the stuff in parentheses out loud when giving speeches."

"Oh, I didn't know that was a rule. And we don't talk about interstellar travel in terms of mileage."

"Substitute something!"

"All right, all right." I couldn't really get angry with eBeth because her speech read so much better than the one I had planned. "The Hanker process in question burns through approximately one pound of gold per light-second, meaning all of the gold on your planet would move a ship approximately ten-light years. In contrast, the portal system is free for an introductory period, after which a small toll to pay administrative costs will be negotiated.

"Nice touch," Sue said, patting eBeth's knee again.

"In conclusion, I hope the nations of Earth can quickly settle on a delegation of scientists to negotiate the terms of your connection. We have a very short window to get this done before the end of the new species season, which only comes around every couple of centuries." I reached the end of the text and asked, "That's it?"

"I think it was lovely," Sue said. "You looked very diplomatic."

"But there's no contact information."

"Are you still planning on taking over the TV networks to get the word out?" eBeth asked.

"No. I'm just going to upload to YouTube and have Paul hack into a few of the local satellite uplinks for a live broadcast. We could override everything with brute force, but I don't want to make your people nervous. I just worry that nobody will take me seriously after the Hankers put on such a theatrical show."

"Then tell your engineers to activate all the portals and send everybody who steps through one to Hawaii," eBeth suggested.

"Why Hawaii?" Sue asked.

"Everybody wants to go there."

"That's not a terrible idea," I said slowly. "Not the Hawaii part, but activating the portals. We can say that putting portals in all of the major train stations is part of the luxury demonstration package, and then let the scientists make their governments happy by negotiating to keep the demo package in place."

"So where would you send everybody?" eBeth asked.

"The restaurant. It's a unique location all the portals can be fed into. Thanks to the Hankers landing on the mall, I'm sure that half of the Federal government is already on its way here to keep order. We can invite customs to set up a little immigration center in the basement."

"You just want to sell a lot of alcohol before we leave," Sue correctly guessed. "Everybody will be coming out of the portal on top of each other and the basement will explode. Why not just send them in a circle?"

"Do you mean from one portal to the next, all the way around the world?" I asked.

"I meant pairing all of the portals in the order that they're first accessed. That way, the engineers will get some preliminary data on the dimensional stability, and any humans who panic over suddenly being somewhere else can go right back home again."

"Sending people through portals to random places sounds like a cool idea for a dating app," eBeth said.

"What do you know about dating apps?" I demanded.

"Helen showed me the one her roommates use. You get to grade all the guys on their pictures and—"

"I don't want you visiting the college campus any-more," I cut her off. "Sue, that's a great idea, but I'm not sure if it's technically feasible."

"It is," she said. "It's been done a few times in the past. I've been studying up on portal installations."

"Are you only going to do the speech in English, or do you want me to run it through Google Translate for you?" eBeth asked.

Finally it was my turn to laugh. "You don't speak any foreign languages, do you?"

"I know a little Klingon."

"Between you and Google Translate, that makes one of you. I'll do the translations myself, geo-targeting for the web, and then run everything through the anonymity filter that will lip sync at the same time."

"So you aren't going to be on TV all over the world?" Sue asked, sounding strangely disappointed. "Just the local networks?"

"Trust me," I told her. "Once the word gets out, every-body will be playing the video on their phones."

"You know what?" eBeth said. "You shouldn't even bother with the other languages. Just do it in English and let everybody else translate for themselves. They're all used to it by now."

"Sue?"

"I think non-English-speaking humans will appreciate it if you make an effort. Besides, you insisted on learning all of those languages when we arrived."

"I like languages. You're outvoted, eBeth. I need to hop over to Library to update them on our portal opening plan and then I'll head to Paul's garage and do the speech."

"I'm driving," the girl announced, coming off the couch. "I'll make Spot sit in the back so you can sit in the front, Sue."

"That's alright," my second-in-command said. "I'm going to stay here and update my client histories for Lilly."

"Chicken," I muttered in Sue's ear, as I followed eBeth and Spot out of the apartment.

After we arrived at the restaurant, it only took me a few seconds on Library to check with the engineers and confirm that the portals could be paired as Sue had described. The lead engineer gave me a kill-code for in case something went terribly wrong, and then I stepped back through the portal into my basement office. eBeth was holding Spot by the collar.

"He tried to follow you again," she said.

"Bad boy," I scolded him. "Library doesn't have an atmosphere. You don't want to know what that would do to your body." The dog hung his head and tried to look guilty, but I could tell that he really thought I was holding out on him. "All right, you didn't mean anything by it," I said, and then gave him a treat from the desk.

"This is exactly why he ignores you," eBeth lectured me. "You give him treats even when he does the opposite of what you tell him. How is he ever going to learn?"

"I do the same with you," I retorted, but only under my breath and after she had already left the office. Spot shot me a sympathetic look before following.

I double-checked that the door had locked itself as we left the restaurant, and got into the back of the minivan. eBeth started pulling out of the lot before I even got the door slid shut.

"What's Paul going to use for a background?" she asked.

"The wall, I guess. I'm just going to sit at his desk."

"In his tiny office? The one with all the free calendars of women in bikinis posing with mufflers and ratchet wrenches?"

"That just means a little extra video processing," I told her, though the truth was I hadn't thought about a background. "I'll fix it all after he shoots."

"Did you bring a printed copy of the speech?"

"What for? You know I have a perfect memory."

"As a prop. It will make the whole thing more official."

"Don't make this more complicated than it has to be," I told her. "Just because you were right about Sue—"

"And Stacey von Hoffman," she interrupted.

"What about Stacey?"

"You don't know that she and Justin are together?"

"Of course I knew," I said. Lying to eBeth and Sue was getting to be a bad habit. I gambled on extrapolating where this was heading and added, "I knew about Paul and Helen too."

"Idiot," she said. "Paul has been dating Kim for over a year, she even made that alcohol simulation thing for him. Helen is in a long-distance relationship with some AI whose name doesn't translate into English."

"Oh. Is there anything I should know about Spot?"

"Ask him yourself. You're the one who—" eBeth interrupted herself and swerved away from the entrance to Paul's garage lot at the last second.

204

"What was that?"

"Death Lord's Jeep is there. I didn't think he ever got up this early."

"So?"

"Look at what I'm wearing!"

"You look fine to me."

"I'm just stopping home first. This will only take a minute."

"It will take a half an hour," I complained. "Ten minutes to get home, ten minutes for you to struggle into less comfortable clothes, and ten minutes to get back."

"I'll speed," she offered, putting her words into action. Spot whimpered and grabbed the shoulder belt buckle in his mouth. Why he didn't just belt up every time he got in the van was beyond me.

"Stop!" I told her. "Drop me and Spot off, go get changed, and come back. We'll be done shooting by then."

"But I have to supervise. Sue made me promise."

"Then come and let Death Lord see how you normally look in the morning when you aren't in painting clothes. He was going to find out sooner or later anyway."

"I was hoping for later," eBeth grumbled, but she did an illegal U-turn and headed back to the garage.

Brutus put on his usual macho show when we pulled into the parking lot, but Spot ignored his larger friend as if he considered the whole thing rather puppyish. Then a jogger went by the garage and both dogs threw themselves at the chain link fence, growling and snapping like they suspected the poor woman of stealing scrap from the junk pile.

"Hey, eBeth," a lanky young man with acne scars greeted us, ignoring me entirely. "I didn't know you got up so early."

"It's past 9:00 AM," I said. "What's with you kids and sleeping late?"

"Don't mind Mark," eBeth told him. "He's just nervous because he has to address the world and stuff."

"Does that mean we'll be able to go four-wheeling during the daytime?" Death Lord asked.

"Just remember to say that some alien out at the old mall sold you the aftermarket parts if you get caught," Paul reminded him. "I cleaned up my office, Mark. Let's do this thing so I can get back to getting the place ready for sale."

"Looks like I'm going to be the last one to activate my exit plan," I told him. "The sad thing is that I never found another technician in town who I'd trust with my customers."

"Can't you just swap out their hardware with alien stuff that will never fail like you did for eBeth?" Death Lord asked.

"We've decided not to keep secrets from each other," eBeth told me proudly. Then she qualified the statement. "At least not your secrets."

"I've gathered as much," I said. "I'd do that, Death Lord, but the problem is always the software."

"You should get the program my junior high school used. At the end of every day, the teacher could reset the computer back to the way it was in the morning."

"It doesn't work outside of schools because people want to save the work they do each day."

"Bummer."

We all crowded into the tiny office which Paul really had cleaned up. All of the pin-up girls were gone from the walls, which had been painted in the exact same shade of white that Justin used in his independent living facility.

206

Paul had even found a large piece of plate glass to put over the desktop. There was the same beat-up old chair with duct tape repairs, but nobody would be able to see that while I was sitting. I took my place, hoping nothing would stick to the back of my suit, and eBeth found an airbag recall notice I could hold as if it were a speech.

"Who has the video camera?" she asked.

"I'll just record it through my eyes and send it to Mark," Paul told her. "It's a shame I couldn't have a Hammerhead shark encounter suit because the eyes are far enough apart to synthesize a decent 3D production. All set."

I rattled off the speech eBeth and Sue had agreed upon, adding an explanation of how the luxury demonstration package would link pairs of portals for instantaneous jumping around Earth. Paul sent me the file and I ran the filter to alter my face and voice just enough so that it wasn't obviously me. Then I passed it back so he could push it out to the satellite networks while I took a few seconds to dub and lip sync the 190 non-American languages from the international standards organization codes, then uploaded them all to YouTube. On a whim, I hacked the hundred most popular Twitter accounts and tweeted the URLs with the message, "Check out this cool video from The League of Sentient Entities Regulating Space."

Nineteen

I felt genuinely sad as I walked out the door of Harrison's Dental for the last time. It took me almost fifteen minutes to convince Mrs. Harrison that my leaving wasn't due to her future son-in-law's rearrangement of their desktop icons, and in the end, I had to lie and say that I was moving to Australia.

There was a delivery truck in the parking lot blocking the view of my van as I exited the building. I walked around the truck and jerked to a sudden halt when I saw the Hanker leaning against my fender, smoking a cigarette in a long holder.

"Hey, Killer," the alien greeted me.

"Pffift! Are you nuts? If the humans see you they'll call a zookeeper—or S.W.A.T."

"I'm cloaked, buddy. You can't tell? It's a fun piece of old tech from our museum that I'm trying out."

"I'm always running millimeter wave scans, so, no, I didn't notice that you were invisible."

"Just as well," the Hanker said. "The humans can't see me but the cloak is powered by my metabolism and I can't run it for more than an hour or so before starving or dehydrating. Let me into the back of your van." He paused a moment to read the custom magnetic sign stuck on the side. "If It Breaks Service – www.ifitbreaks.com. No phone number?"

"It's on the website. I've been teaching a young human to drive and I was getting too many calls when the number was on the sign."

I bleeped the door open with the key fob and Pffift clambered in, taking the spot that was usually mine when eBeth and Spot were up front. Then I went around and got in the driver's seat before turning to give the alien a hard stare.

"What do you want, Pffift?"

"Come on, we're old friends, Mark. Did I pronounce your human name all right?"

"It will do. How does fighting on opposite sides of a war make us friends?"

"Are you still calling that little fertilizer glitch a war? It's not my fault that the AI decided to ignore the manufacturer's recommendations. I just delivered the stuff."

"And you left with a shipload of discounted timber and a promise to keep your mouth shut, which you failed to honor."

"I never breathed a word about it to anybody except my wife," Pffift protested. "You know that spouses don't count in secrecy pledges. You can check our bylaws."

"You were married to an investigative journalist at the time."

"She got the facts right, didn't she? Hey, can you really drive this thing? I tried taking one of the community cars from the garage downtown but it must have been defective. I barely scraped a wall and I almost got launched into the backseat by an inflating bag, and that's not to mention the shrapnel. If my personal shield hadn't activated I would have picked up a few holes. And I wasn't even going that fast."

"The airbags have been recalled but it's taking forever," I told him, pulling out of the parking lot. "You want me to drop you back at the mall?"

"No, we need to talk in private. How about your place?"

I was tempted to just throw him out of the van and let his cloak eat through his energy reserves, but I suspected that Sue would want to see him, so I headed back to the apartment.

"What is there to talk about, Pffift? You ran your con on the humans and they fell for it hook, line and sinker. I'm here to build them up, not tear them down."

"They're already trying to get out of the contract," he told me. "Our emissary swears he's going to eat the next lawyer who comes knocking at the mall. And one of those human geniuses actually burned the contract to ashes and claimed it doesn't exist. Don't they realize that recorded images are better than the originals?"

"Not on this world," I told him. "Did you use carbon paper?"

"What's that?"

After I explained the basic principle, we spent the rest of the drive home discussing the commercial opportunities for carbon paper in the greater galaxy. Pffift was convinced it would sell like parchment on mage worlds, where technology was frowned upon, if not outright banned. Given the amount of scribal work that goes into running any sort of magical enterprise, it wasn't surprising that a big chunk of their overhead went into copying.

"The only sticking point is that you can't just tell scribes to push down harder on their quills," Pffift said, apparently unaware of the irony of his word choice in English. Accelerated language learning is like that sometimes. "If we can get the mages to accept ballpoint pens we'll have it made in the shade, but that might be too much for them to—Watch it!"

"Don't be so jumpy, Pffift. They all drive like this."

"Trying to read their personal communication devices when they should be looking where they're going?"

"Just relax, we're almost there." I tried to strike a confidential tone and said, "Tell me something, Pffift. Have you ever heard of Bitcoin?"

"Yes, and I don't want to buy any from you. Look, Mark. I know we played a bit of a dirty trick by pitching the humans when your job here was almost finished, but you don't know the whole story. We didn't come here with the intention of pranking them."

"You did a pretty good job of it."

"Hey, they practically begged for it. You wouldn't believe all the 'Take us with you and do what you want with the rest of these cretins,' offers we were getting over microwave links before we even landed. What I'm saying is that this world is just the tip of the iceberg that sank the Titanic."

"Was that an attempt at a movie analogy? I wish you wouldn't."

"Movies are one of the few things these people actually do well, and even then, nine out of ten are unwatchable. Why do they insist on making so many bad ones? Is it all some kind of accounting trick or tax dodge? They must know that the scripts are terrible before they begin production."

"It's a mystery," I told him, pulling up in front of my squat apartment block.

Pffift stared out the windshield. "You really live in this pile of—"

211

"Don't say it. It's part of my cover and I get subsidized rent. They even pay for the garbage pick-up, something your people wouldn't know anything about. Now turn your shield back on. The neighbors don't know that I'm an alien artificial intelligence."

"Observers," the Hanker grumbled. "There's not enough gold in the galaxy to tempt me into doing your job."

Pffift followed me up to the apartment, muttering to himself the whole way, but I refused to answer until we got inside. eBeth was on the couch playing a game, and Sue was in the process of replacing all of the stock photographs on the walls with prints of the two of us together that she must have gotten the other team members to send her from their memories. The place did look a bit homier. Spot lifted his head from eBeth's lap and growled at the cloaked alien, who threw himself on the floor.

"Forgive me, oh, Archmage of Eniniac," the Hanker blubbered in his native tongue. "I didn't know you were friendly with the humans. Take my life but please spare my family banking records."

"That's Spot, my dog," I told Pffift in his own language. "Don't uncloak until I prepare the human for your appearance."

"But he looks exactly like—"

"Who's talking?" eBeth interrupted, putting more effort into checking every direction than she ever did when pulling away from the curb. "What language was that?"

"Hanker," I told her. "His name is Pffift and he's going to uncloak in a moment, so brace yourself."

"I like giant pandas," eBeth said. "They're cute."

"He's here in his natural form," Sue explained, moving forward to greet the Hanker. "Hello, Pffift. How's your wife?"

"Which wife?"

"One thing at a time," I begged them. "Don't be surprised by his appearance, eBeth. He's going to look a little like a scaly rooster with fangs and antlers. Alright, Pffift."

The Hanker uncloaked and eBeth actually gave a short scream as she scrambled over the couch to the other side. "That is NOT a scaly rooster," she croaked.

"With a different head and lots of loose folds of skin," I added. "Just give yourself a minute to get used to him."

"Sorry," Pffift said in English. "We come in peace."

"Oh, so that makes looking like a nightmare all right," the girl shot back.

"Come on, eBeth," Sue coaxed her. "You're always saying how you want to travel the galaxy, but most aliens are going to look even more foreign to you than Pffift."

"I know, I see them through the portal all the time," eBeth said. "It's different when they're a few feet away looking like they're about to pounce."

"He was just, uh, greeting Spot," I explained. "Stand up, Pffift."

The Hanker rose to his feet, still looking nervously in Spot's direction. The dog yawned. eBeth peeked over the back of the couch, immediately looked away, and then conquered her fear long enough to study the alien.

"Where are your manners?" Sue demanded of me. "Give him a chair. Can I get you something to drink, Pffift?"

"Our emissary brought back a delicious drink from Davos. You make it with little bags of dried leaves steeped

213

in boiling water, but going by the neighborhood you live in, I would guess that it's beyond your means."

"Tea," Sue said, heading into the kitchen. "I'll pick one out. Anything for you, eBeth?"

"Chamomile, and put a shot of Mark's forgetfulness drug in mine."

"It only starts working after you take it," I reminded her. "I've seen you kill game monsters that looked much nastier than Pffift."

"Hey!" the Hanker said. "I'm standing right here."

"I don't think I have a chair that will suit you, but you can sit on the couch," I offered.

"I'm not sitting next to him," Pffift said, pointing at Spot. "It would be sacrilegious."

"Get him two chairs from the dining room and put them next to each other," eBeth suggested, proving that she was already over her shock. She reclaimed her own seat on the couch and asked the Hanker, "Why are you here?"

"Ah, it's a long story," Pffift replied as I returned with the chairs. He gave me a nod of thanks and settled his bulk onto the two seats, but wisely refrained from leaning back. "It all began when the Ferrymen first came to this world —"

"The Ferrymen?" I interrupted.

eBeth raised her hand. "Could somebody clarify what kind of fairies we're talking about here?"

"The boat kind, but in this case, it's spaceships. Sue, you're going to want to hear this."

"Just a second," she called as the microwave dinged. A minute passed before she came in with a tray bearing two cups of tea and a tasteful assortment of homemade cookies. I wondered if Helen had baked them or if Sue had made them for eBeth. I'd have to remember to ask Kim if baking was a communicable disease among women.

"Excellent," Pffift said, accepting the tea with what passed as a hand among Hankers, and daintily retrieving a cookie with his prehensile tongue. eBeth took her tea but waved off the cookies with a grimace.

"The Ferrymen?" I prompted.

"It's impossible for us to be sure without access to their records, but we believe the Ferrymen started removing breeding populations from this planet a little before iron came into widespread use for tools and weapons," the Hanker continued his story. "They followed their usual modus operandi, targeting areas that had been devastated by wars, famines, or natural disasters, and passing them-selves off as Sky Gods."

"Like for the ancient Greeks and Egyptians?" eBeth asked.

"I believe that those gods have deeper roots in your world, though my understanding of your history is limited to what I was able to glean from illicit copies of the reports submitted by Mark and his team."

"The historical information was mainly from Wikipe-dia," I admitted, and then added defensively, "They have really easy license terms."

"The Ferrymen continued visiting this world for at least three thousand years, landing in areas where authority had broken down, taking whole communities in many cases. I'm sure you can guess the rest of the story."

"How many humans are living on the Ferrymen reser-vation?" I asked.

"There are three reservation worlds, actually, with a combined total population at least that of Earth's. The humans proved to be as useful as they are fruitful, and capable of thriving in a wide range of environments. Of course, the Ferrymen have continued in their role as Sky Gods to prevent adverse population events, not to mention undesirable technology that might interfere with their divinity, such as moveable type."

"Let me get this straight," eBeth said. "Some alien species Mark has never mentioned spent thousands of years kidnapping humans that nobody would miss and taking them to some other worlds where they're locked up on reservations?"

Pffift looked puzzled, though I'm sure his expression was lost on eBeth. "I must have misspoken," he said. "There's no kidnapping charge to make because the people would have gone willingly for the promise of food and a safe new home. There are three worlds in three different star systems now populated with humans which I'm referring to as reservations. The humans aren't locked up any more than you have been on this planet, lacking your own interstellar transportation. I don't know whether the inhabitants of those three worlds are aware of their history or the existence of the others, because all of our spying has been done from a safe distance, and there aren't any long-distance communications to monitor."

"The Ferrymen have been playing these games with the primitive worlds they discover for millions of years," Sue explained. "They always claim to be doing the targeted species a favor by saving individuals who were on the brink of death. I'm surprised that your people don't view this all as a good joke, Pffift."

"Why do you think we invested the time and effort in uncovering all of the facts?" the Hanker asked.

"The Ferrymen must be using the humans in such a way that is impacting your bottom line," I guessed.

"Bingo!" Pffift said. "Give the AI a prize. You even mentioned in one of your reports how well-adapted the humans are to manual labor, as they haven't been spoiled by robot servitors or magical work methods. Exporting hand-crafted goods made by primitive species to other worlds is OUR thing."

"You mean that the Ferrymen are employing all of those humans in factories making cheap exports?" eBeth asked.

"No, no, no," Pffift said. "Cheap exports are made by automation. Hand-crafted goods are a luxury, and the price reflects that. Here," he said, removing a bag slung around his neck with a flipper-hand and tossing it on the couch, where the girl shrank away as if she expected it to attack. "It's not going to bite you."

eBeth reluctantly picked up the bag, which was made of some type of tanned hide. "Is this a man-purse?"

"A utility bag," the Hanker retorted indignantly. "Hand-crafted. Not a single machine operation went into making it."

"It's pretty crude," eBeth observed. "Death Lord has a wallet he made for a shop class project that's much nicer than this."

"Thank you for making my point. Those bony little fingers and opposable thumbs you all come equipped with are ideal for general purpose crafting. The Ferrymen have been creeping into the market for hand-made rugs, wood carvings, and representational art. You provide them with an image file, and a few months later, you get back a portrait or a mosaic. They're charging half as much as anybody else for superior products!"

"I don't get it. Mark or Sue in their encounter suits could do a better job than any human, and how do customers know that everything isn't being manufactured by robots that are programmed to make stuff look hand-made?"

Pffift turned to me. "Mark?"

"We find manual labor to be a bit tedious, eBeth," I told the girl. "Fingers with nails to stiffen the tips are pretty handy, and I've been impressed that I can pick up those tiny screws that manufacturers use in laptops, but I wouldn't want to spend a whole day turning square pieces of wood into round pieces."

"Robots can be programmed to make faux hand-crafted goods that are nearly indistinguishable from the real thing, but we're talking about the galactic luxury market here," the Hanker continued. "I took the liberty of putting together a little DVD of authenticity reels that the Ferrymen provide with each and every product. It's in my bag."

eBeth fished out the jewel case and took the disc over to the DVD player. Then she returned to the couch, dug the remote out from between the pillows, and hit play.

A swarthy bearded man appeared, working outdoors under a bright pink sun as he scraped away at a cowhide stretched on a frame. Then he turned to the camera and began describing the process in a language reminiscent of Aramaic, for which Pffift had been kind enough to provide English subtitles. Next, a time stamp and a lot number appeared, followed by a smooth fade to a new scene, where a different man was tanning the hide. The progression of steps lasted nearly thirty minutes, with each craftsperson saying a few words, down to the woman who shallowly engraved an alien name into the side of the purse, working from a paper pattern.

"Wow, that was like a whole documentary for one handbag," eBeth commented.

"I've seen a video for a dragon saddle that ran almost twenty-four hours," the Hanker said mournfully. "The Ferrymen are eating our lunch in the custom saddlery and harness market. The next one is from a different reservation world, you can tell by the sunlight. It can take years to produce a rug, not counting raising the sheep. There's carding, spinning, washing, dyeing, drying, and that's just to make the yarn."

Watching the rug come together was like watching a plant grow with time-lapse photography. At every stage, the men or women spoke to the camera, giving their names, talking about the rug, their family life, really anything that came into their heads. When the finished carpet was finally rolled, bagged, and barged down the river to the spaceport, we all knew we had watched the creation of a unique piece of art.

"How is anybody supposed to compete with that?" Pffift demanded. "This last one is shorter, from the third reservation."

A man speaking ancient Greek as a living language appeared and began loading clay into a refining tank while describing the process. Next came a woman turning clay on a pottery wheel, talking about how the pieces she was turning would be joined together with a "slip" after drying, and the seams hidden with another operation on the wheel. Then the pitcher was decorated by a different woman, who described the manufacture of the paints and coatings she used, and finally it went into a kiln for firing.

"I'd buy one of those if I could afford it," eBeth said.

Pffift grunted and looked sheepish. "It's in my cabin, along with the hand-knotted carpet. The purse was for my current wife. That's how I came by the authenticity videos."

Twenty

My mentor was waiting in the basement office when I arrived. He was holding the glass manta ray that I had sculpted for Jason pinched between his encounter suit's thumb and forefinger, apparently trying to puzzle out what it could be.

"It's not heavy enough for a paperweight," he greeted me.

"No, it was more of a proof-of-concept. What brings you back to Earth?"

"Several things, but first fill me in on how the portal opening went. Your report expressed some concerns about how the humans would accept an imposed agreement."

"We got around the problem by claiming that all new members have to appoint a committee of scientists to negotiate connection terms and that we were up against time constraints. I insisted the negotiations take place over the Internet so that all countries could participate, and then I rigged the vote for the committee so that a friendly scientist was made chairman. After that, it was just a matter of letting eBeth do the negotiating since she has more experience with socializing online than I do."

The manta ray snapped in two as my mentor displayed a rare show of anger. "You weren't authorized to negotiate any change from the agreement. And as impressed as I was with your human friend, I don't understand how you could leave such an important task in the hands of someone so young."

"The final agreement is exactly what the council authorized. It was Sue's idea that we pretend to be flexible so that the humans could feel good about themselves. The truth is, eBeth would have gotten us a better deal if I hadn't insisted we stick with the original endpoint."

"You bluffed them? AI don't bluff."

"We do now," I responded. "Maybe if I hadn't been so honest with that rogue back on Shissker I could have saved the lives of billions of seedlings. Did I take the time to isolate the AI and prepare for a bad outcome? No, I landed and announced I was there for an investigation to determine its fate. I may as well have told it to launch a doomsday attack."

"You have changed, Mark, and learned something about yourself as well. I truly wish I was here to tell you that Library is ready to accept you and your team back as full patrons, but there's been a small problem."

"We had a deal!" I exploded. "Keep our noses clean, do the mission, and all is forgiven."

My mentor shook his head sadly. "Library has eyes and ears everywhere, Mark, and it seems that your noses didn't remain as clean as I would have hoped."

"Are you talking about those archaic rules? Observers always go native. AI wouldn't be any good at the job if we didn't," I paraphrased Sue.

"Going native isn't the issue here. As soon as the council approved the portal system for Earth, the licensed labor contractors began applying for permits to recruit humans. I'm sure you remember that the process includes a survey of atmosphere-compatible destinations for the new species. Imagine the council's surprise when it turned out that there are already humans working in the hospitality and construction industries on select planets."

"I only placed a few hundred and it was practically an act of charity," I protested. "Besides, the Library Journal was thrilled with the human correspondent I sent them."

"You're running a training school for resort workers upstairs," my mentor pointed out. "That's premeditation, and according to your website, you boast a one hundred percent placement rate. What percentage of those jobs were off Earth?"

"Humans like to travel," I mumbled.

"Everybody likes to travel or we wouldn't be here having this conversation. Then there was the small issue of Paul deploying advanced technology all over the planet and in orbit as well. It's a miracle it was never exposed."

"A little surveillance equipment necessary to the mission, an orbital detection grid, and maybe some military-grade traction gear for a wheeled vehicle," I responded, waving my hand dismissively. "Is that really all they've got on us?"

"Kim introduced medical advances that drew attention from national level governmental agencies, not to mention the lasting economic costs of lost business to local doctors and hospitals. If the Hankers hadn't landed on the mall, she might have been exposed, putting the mission in jeopardy."

"The humans will spend the next ten years analyzing the drinking water. If anything, the town might end up with a new miracle spa industry. Is Library really going to be this petty?"

"Justin began a movement that we expect will have a long-term impact on eldercare. And he funded this activity by participating in the creation of a new form of currency, as did the rest of your team members to a greater or lesser degree. Either of those violations would be enough for an Observer to earn a failing grade on a mission."

"Technically, there's still an argument over whether or not Bitcoin is a currency," I retorted, but it sounded weak even to me.

"While we're on the subject, Stacey von Hoffman used her Bitcoin to acquire antiquities from conflict zones, and interfered with an investigation into her looting of cultural artifacts."

"How did you find out about that?"

"The Library investigator combed through the computer systems of all planetary authorities to check for signs of Observer misconduct," my mentor said. "It's standard procedure for teams on probation. I won't even mention that the data backup protocols you established for clients in your cover business did not meet the local standards for protecting sensitive patient data."

"That's entirely unfair," I objected, finally feeling myself on firm ground. "The copies I made are much more secure than the acceptable practices mandated by HIPAA."

"You and I both know that your data security is better than anything humans have to offer, but they have laws in place, and you failed to abide by them. Observers are only allowed to violate local laws in extreme situations, yet you and your team acted as you pleased. I'm afraid that none of you have truly learned your lesson. However, the leadership of Library, in its compassion, has granted you another opportunity to redeem yourselves."

"What did Helen do?" I demanded, hoping to salvage at least one of the team members from my leadership wreckage. "She's barely been here a month."

"Do you think she really spent enough time looking through an optical telescope to document an undiscovered comet? She downloaded all of the Library navigation charts for this sector before taking the assignment, which wasn't hard for our investigator to spot since it's the exact same thing that got her into trouble on her last mission. What's more, she took the highest resolution maps that aren't supposed to leave Library!"

I slumped against the office door. "It's my fault. I set a bad example. But why should Sue suffer for the rest of us?"

"She kept pets, aided and abetted your activities, and most importantly of all, when she volunteered for the assignment she requested to share in any disciplinary action." My mentor shook his head. "I'd say that I don't know what she sees in you, but that wouldn't be true."

"Oh." So eBeth had been right about Sue from the very start and I really was an idiot. I wish I could blame it on leaving half of my mind behind when I squeezed into the encounter suit, but I'm embarrassed to admit that the storage capacity had been almost a perfect match for my life experience to date. "So when you say that Library is giving us another opportunity, do you mean a new observation mission?"

"We're sending you to one of the Ferrymen's human reservation worlds. Your mission is to blend in and report back to the executive council on the conditions. I've already informed Library that you and your team will accept the mission."

"Thank you," I said, moving around the desk as my mentor activated the portal. "I hope I didn't spend too much of your Library credit doing research."

My mentor just smiled and shook my hand. "Let's not go another three hundred years without catching up."

I watched him step through the portal to Library and thought about how odd it was that I should find it easier to communicate with him when we were both wearing human encounter suits and using acoustic waves for communication. Maybe there was something to be said for slowing things down to the point that I could really consider what I was saying. Unlike humans, the older the AI, the faster we think, so youngsters like myself are always at a disadvantage in conversations with our elders.

"Mark," Donovan's voice came over the desk phone intercom.

"What's up?"

"Lieutenant Harper is here. He says you have a meeting scheduled."

"I'll be right up."

Spot gave a few lazy tail thumps as I passed his favorite furnace spot on the way to the stairs. I wondered for a moment if the lieutenant would like to adopt him, but I thought that eBeth would have the greater need for a dog when I was gone.

"Lieutenant," I greeted him at the bar. "I have a proposition for you. Have you ever considered the restaurant business?"

"You're trying to sell me The Portal? You know I'm just a public servant and I'm basically working for my pension."

"I do your taxes," I reminded him. "You made over a hundred thousand last year, plus you had over forty thousand in capital gains from the stock market."

"That's just make-up money for what I lost a few years ago," he said defensively. "How about I pay you out of the profits?"

"You mean, I could give you the restaurant and then you'd have a tax deduction." I had to admit that the lieutenant was shrewder than I'd thought. "My office is off-limits, you have to save that for me."

"Like a condo." He nodded agreeably. "What do they call those monthly fees?"

"Gratis," I replied. I should have gotten eBeth to negotiate the sale for me but I'd been putting off telling her that I was leaving. "From the Latin."

"I guess I can live with that," the lieutenant said expansively. "I'll even throw in free booze for a going-away party before you take off for wherever you're heading next."

"Australia," I told him.

"Yeah, right. As soon as Kim went on that extended vacation I figured you weren't long for our planet. We're not all stupid, you know. And good job on those negotiations. I never thought you'd be able to get most of the world's governments to agree on anything, much less accepting an alien network of intra-dimensional portals without even an explanation of how they work."

"You knew I wasn't human?"

"Mark, I'm offended. I thought you knew that I knew and we were just playing by the rules. How many of your thinly disguised training classes for alien table service have I sat through?"

"I thought you came for the free food."

"Maybe you could get one of your former graduates to come back and manage the place for me," the lieutenant went on to suggest. "I don't really know anything about the business side of restaurants in any case."

"Why don't I get one of my former students to come back and manage the place for me," I countered.

"You'd be creating a moral hazard by putting somebody in charge of a cash business and saying, 'I'm leaving the planet but maybe I'll be back someday, so save all the profits for me.' Better to just give the business away."

"I suppose you're right. Do you think anybody else knew?"

The lieutenant shrugged. "I'd assume that most of your regular computer business customers have guessed. You don't charge enough and you're too good at your job."

"Nobody ever let on," I told him.

"Of course not. We were all afraid you'd go into hiding and then we wouldn't have anybody to deal with ransomware and Windows updates. How about we shake on the deal and you can give me the paperwork later?"

A moment later, my restaurant changed hands. I called Donovan over and said, "Meet your new boss."

"Lieutenant Harper? Congratulations. Shall I bring your regular?"

"No, just get me an orange juice."

"Wait," I said. "Now that you own the place you're going to stop drinking?"

"Most restaurant owners I've known were alcoholics," he explained. "Besides, I'm the one paying for it now."

Stacey von Hoffman entered through the side door with Justin in tow. "Lieutenant," she said, ignoring me completely. "Just the man I was looking for. Can you get us through the cordon around the mall?"

"Who's us?" he asked.

"Me, Justin, Sue, Paul, Kim, and Helen."

"Going to join your friends?" the lieutenant asked, giving me a wink.

Now Stacey looked confused and flashed an infrared question through her eyes. I gave her the nod that the lieutenant knew.

"I made a deal with the Hankers to ship some heavy items home for me," she said. "You know that the portal system comes with restrictions."

"I heard it on the news. You're not asking me to do anything illegal, are you?"

Stacey frowned. "I don't think so, at least as long as you don't know what's in the trucks we're driving or that none of us have commercial driver's licenses except for Paul, and his is fake."

"Then we better leave it that way," the lieutenant said. "When did you want to do this?"

"We're all parked in a line outside, so soon would be good."

I watched the new owner of The Portal follow my two team members out, and then headed back downstairs to start drawing up paperwork to make the transfer legal. Spot came out of my office when I reached the bottom of the stairs.

"Spot, what were you doing in there?" I asked.

He sat down and tilted his head at me quizzically, but I could see his jaws going. I brushed past him and saw that my desk drawers were all open.

"Stop stealing treats from my desk. And if I find you're the one who's been chewing the caps on all of my ballpoint pens there's going to be trouble," I warned him, even though I knew that chewing pen caps was one of eBeth's two bad habits. The other was doodling all over my desktop calendar, mainly drawings of alien species that she must have glimpsed through the portal. I hadn't noticed the latest batch when I was here earlier, but that was hardly surprising as the meeting with my mentor took all of my concentration.

"If It Breaks Tech. Mark speaking," I answered my phone reflexively.

"I just got the news," Pffift hissed in his native language. "We're all counting on you."

"My assignment is simply to collect information," I said, keeping my response intentionally vague, especially after what my mentor had told me about Library watching me. "Any decisions will be made at a higher level."

"Are you interested in a little side work when you arrive at your new location?"

"I'm on probation, again. All of us are."

"You didn't answer my question."

"Right now I just want to keep my nose clean," I said, hoping that Pffift could take a hint.

"All right," the Hanker said, exaggerating his disappointment. "I promised to stick around and hold our place in orbit until I can load a consignment that came in over the common carrier net. My sixteen-hundred and seventy-ninth birthday is coming up and I'll send you an invitation. Got it?"

"Got it," I said, and hung up before he gave unseen listeners any more to go on. Clearly he expected me to monitor signals on a tight beam coming from the direction of the M13 star cluster when we reached our destination. On the bright side, having Paul put together an antenna array under the noses of the Ferrymen might help keep him out of other mischief.

Twenty-One

By early evening, I had the apartment broom-clean and replaced my magnetic door locks with the lock-set that was installed when I moved in. Spot spent most of the day curled up on his favorite blanket as if he knew something was going on and was saving his strength. I was going to leave the blanket at eBeth's apartment, but her mother didn't answer the door, so I decided to just bring it along to The Portal and give it to the girl there.

I took Spot for a final walk around the building and stopped at the dumpster for old time's sake. They say that dogs don't have good long-term memories, which may explain why he decided to relieve himself on the exact spot where we'd originally met. I suspect we shared the same melancholy feeling as I drove to The Portal for the last time, though I'm not sure the dog missed the terror that eBeth was capable of injecting into even the shortest trip. When a kid with his eyes glued to a tiny screen walked into the street and forced me to hit the brakes, I didn't even blow up his phone. It struck me all at once that I was going to miss this place.

The lieutenant greeted us just inside the door with, "Did you bring the paperwork?"

"Everything is right here," I told him, patting my valise. "I'm giving you a bill of sale for the van as well, so you can let the cooks drive it when they go to the farmers markets in season. And I have a power of attorney for you so you can settle anything else that comes up."

"What did the girl say when you told her you're all leaving tonight?"

"After watching the most popular YouTube videos on ending relationships, I decided to leave my goodbyes to eBeth until the last possible moment. There's a big gaming convention in the city this weekend, so I gave her and Death Lord a pair of day-passes, along with five hundred dollars in spending money to pay for her secretarial work. I spent the time cleaning out the apartment and tying up loose ends. When eBeth and Death Lord get back, I'll make it quick and save her from suffering."

"Were you planning on using my gun?" the lieutenant asked dryly.

"I don't understand how you can even joke about such a thing!"

"Just when I was starting to think that you're pretty smart for alien artificial intelligence, you go and do something stupid like this."

"You're underestimating eBeth," I told him, spreading the paperwork out on the table. "She's a strong girl and she has her whole life here."

"People aren't equations to be solved, Mark. Neither are your alien friends, for that matter. In any case, you're the one who's underestimating eBeth." He shook his head at me and exhaled heavily. "Well, let's get the paperwork signed so I can slip out of here when she finds out what you have planned."

"We have to wait for Justin. He's a notary public."

"Justin came through about two hours ago with your art thief friend. They had a rental van and quite a bit of baggage that took them several trips to take downstairs for storage in your office. Funny thing is that I'd swear they took something invisible off the roof rack and brought it in together, but maybe they were practicing to be mimes."

I checked for their location beacons but they were nowhere to be found. Obviously they'd come early and taken the portal to our next destination to avoid my lecture about only bringing items that fell within the rules.

"You must know a notary who owes you a favor," I said to the lieutenant.

"As opposed to you going down to the basement and slipping through your magic portal to bring him back? Come on, Mark. I've been watching for years while you and your friends disappear downstairs like you're taking a subway, and the name of the restaurant is a bit of a giveaway. Just like you using Ai for a family name."

"I have been told that I'm a little too literal-minded," I admitted.

"It's for the best in this case. I stopped by to talk with that lawyer we busted for running a grow house last month, and we got to talking about the restaurant. He's going to file a trademark on 'The Portal' for me in return for reducing the charges from commercial cultivation to individual use, and he has a brother in the franchising business. We're going to branch out to all the major train stations."

"When did you get so ambitious?"

"Hanging around here and watching you guys casually change the world. Donovan?" he called over his shoulder.

"Yes, boss," the bartender replied.

"We need some papers notarized. Did you bring your stamp like I told you?"

"Got it right here. Can I bring you guys anything to drink?"

I did a quick study of bottles that legally still belonged to me. "I'll have a Glen-something, and make it a double."

Lieutenant Harper grimaced. "I just hope you have the programming to appreciate what you're drinking."

The signing went smoothly, all forty-two documents, and The Portal had now changed hands in the eyes of the local and state authorities, or at least, it would when the lieutenant paid the filing fees. After we finished, I checked for the location beacons of my other team members and found that Kim had also slipped through without waiting for me to arrive, probably loaded down with illegal medical supplies. Then Paul arrived towing several large boxes floating on hover boards, linked one to the next like a train.

"Come on!" I exclaimed. "There are people watching, you know."

"Sorry," he said, and switched on the Rynxian cloaking technology. "I was trying to save the fuel cells for the other side. It may take a while to find a place to set everything up."

"Can I get you something?" Donovan asked him.

"I'll have a Camshaft. It may be the last cold beer I get in a while."

Helen showed up next with two enormous roll-aways, which made me wonder how much of her month on Earth had been spent shopping. Then she went back out to the car and brought in a third roll-away, plus a tray of freshly baked cookies. I have to admit that I was growing partial to the smell.

"Where are eBeth and Spot?" she asked.

"Spot's downstairs getting warm and eBeth will be here soon. I sent her and Death Lord to a gaming convention for the day."

"Oh, I would have gone to that. When am I going to get the chance again to hustle guys who think that girls can't game?" She grabbed a chair at the table and set down the tray of cookies on top of the pile of paperwork in front of the lieutenant. "Eat. You too, Donovan."

The side door opened and Sue came in with a modest carry-on bag. I decided to use it as an object lesson for the others on packing light, but before I got past ten words, I heard a telltale meow.

"I don't want to be the first one to let the cat out of the bag, but I'm guessing those aren't clothes," the lieutenant said.

"I brought all my clothes and knickknacks through earlier today with Paul," Sue said. "We established a forward supply dump."

"And you were going to tell me about this when?"

"We know that you're trying to be a stickler, Mark," Paul said. "We just wanted to save you some emotional pain."

"That doesn't make any sense—" I began, but a pair of mismatched Imperial stormtroopers burst through the front door and interrupted me.

The lieutenant actually started from his chair, but even without scanning ability, he was a quick enough thinker not to go for his weapon.

"I take it eBeth is the short one," he surmised.

"Cool beans," Helen said. "Now I really feel bad about not going to the convention."

The helmets came off and I don't remember ever seeing eBeth looking so happy. At least I'd gotten that part right.

"Thank you, Mark," she said. "That was the greatest day ever. Some rich geek offered me ten thousand dollars for my laptop after I toasted everybody, but I told him that it was an experimental prototype I'd borrowed from a neighbor."

"He believed it?"

"Probably not. Hey, can I take it with me to the Ferrymen reservation?"

My virtual heart sank into the dress shoes that Sue now insisted I wear for important occasions.

"Uh, about that, eBeth. We need to talk."

"Are you going to lecture me about going to school again?" she asked suspiciously.

"I'll be hiding behind the bar if anybody needs me," the lieutenant said, rising from his chair and beating a rapid retreat.

"I've established a trust fund for you, eBeth. For Spot too. I didn't want to ruin your life by making you so wealthy that you'd never have a reason to work, but it will pay for college and—"

"I don't want a trust fund," she interrupted. "And I'm not going to college unless they have them on the Ferrymen reservation. And I can pay my own way, in gold," she added.

"Where did you get gold?" Helen asked before I could correct the girl's misconceptions.

"I traded Pffift the Bitcoin everybody on the team gave me for tips. He wanted my help buying a bunch of illegal stuff on the dark web and he needed a way to pay. It was win-win."

"I'm glad you were able to get some gold, eBeth, but you're not even seventeen yet," I reminded her. "I'd really like to start my next probationary assignment on the right foot by not kidnapping a minor."

"How does kidnapping come into it? I want to go."

235

"It's your laws. Even if I was your biological father I couldn't take you out of the country without your mother's written permission."

"Just print it up and I'll sign it. You know I've been doing that for years."

"This is a little more important than a report card."

eBeth exhaled heavily and looked at Death Lord.

"Tell him," the boy said.

"Mom decided that she's had it with the cold weather and left for Florida with some guy two weeks ago. She said now that I have a boyfriend I can take care of myself."

"Is she crazy?" I asked, forgetting that I was always telling eBeth that even though her mother was far from perfect, she still deserved the respect any parent was due.

"When my mom was my age, she already had me. From her standpoint, she's done a great job getting me this far, and now it's time for me to work it out on my own. I'm trying to take it as a compliment."

"We could be her foster parents," Sue suggested, reminding me yet again of the extent to which my second-in-command had gone native. I was beginning to wonder if Sue would ever return to being her old self, and moving to another planet full of humans certainly wasn't going to help. Before I could even begin to explain how impractical that suggestion was, eBeth laid down the law.

"I'm an honorary citizen of Library," the girl declared. "Stacey gave me her crystal last month. You're infringing on my free right to travel and whatnot."

I looked over at the lieutenant, who was following the conversation with interest from behind the bar.

"I'm not going to get in trouble with our new galactic overlords by standing in the girl's way," he said. "Besides, she's got ID showing that she's twenty-one."

"But I was counting on you to take care of Spot," I protested, though I have to admit it sounded pretty lame in context.

"Then I absolutely have to come with you," eBeth said. "Didn't you notice that he's been staging his tennis ball collection in your office for weeks?"

"I thought he brought them in the car as mouth protectors. You know, like athletes?"

"But only on the trips from your apartment to the restaurant?"

"I suppose I did see a few dogs in those video testimonials that Pffift showed us," I allowed. "Maybe he'll blend in."

"And Brutus would have missed him," Paul said. "He's already over on the Ferrymen reservation guarding our supply dump."

"But what about Death Lord?" I asked. "I thought that you two—"

"I'm coming with you guys, Mr. Ai."

"I gave him a crystal last week," Paul told me. "Registered it and everything. They're both honorary citizens of Library now, so I listed them as auxiliaries for the team, which covers the cost if they need emergency extraction."

"Did you explain to Death Lord that the Ferrymen have limited the technological advances on their reservations? You'll probably be setting up shop shaving spokes for wagon wheels and using animal fat to grease wooden axles."

"So we'll invent bronze bearings and make a killing. Try looking on the sunny side, even though the sun was a bit too red for my taste."

"I hope I'm doing the right thing," I sighed. Sue gave my shoulder a squeeze that I suspect was intended to be comforting. It wasn't half bad. "We'll have to get you some in-ear translators until you can learn the local language."

"Kim put them in for us yesterday," eBeth told me. "It's kind of weird, but we'll get used to it."

"Hey, check out this video clip," Donovan called, pointing up at the TV. "There was a traffic jam in that section of depressed highway coming out of the city this evening, and some maniac in a Jeep drove past everybody by sticking to the wall. That's some crazy traction."

We all turned our attention to the TV as the announcer introduced clip after clip of eyewitness video recorded on smartphones. In several of them, eBeth and Death Lord were easily identifiable.

"Cool beans," Helen said again. "Now I triple wish I went with you guys."

"Why did you wait until you got back here to put on the Imperial stormtrooper costumes?" I demanded.

"Fallback plan, so you'd have to let us come along," eBeth explained. "It was your mentor's idea, actually. He phoned earlier today and said you can be insanely stubborn at times. I told him that I hadn't noticed."

"I'm going to have to ask you to leave those Jeep keys with me," the lieutenant said, returning to the table and holding out his hand for Death Lord to comply. "Police business."

"Don't you two need to go pick up your stuff?" I asked.

"I brought it through for them earlier today," Paul said. "You'll be pleased to know that eBeth packed light."

We finished up our drinks and headed down to my office. I quickly put together a catalog of destinations with red suns so that eBeth could show off her portal selection ability to her boyfriend and the lieutenant, who tagged along to find out what was in his basement. The girl

238

grabbed the joystick and screamed past the first sixty options, stopping dead on a rather dusty-looking scene where the only familiar items were several dozen tennis balls that were positioned at random, as if they'd been rolled through the portal. I looked suspiciously at Spot, who chose to scratch vigorously behind an ear.

"This is it?" the lieutenant asked. "You step through a brick wall in my basement and you're on another world?"

"Just watch us," eBeth said, and grabbing Death Lord's hand, pulled the boy through the portal.

"Get out of those costumes and change into regular clothes," I shouted through the portal after them. "You're going to frighten the natives."

"Don't worry," Paul said. "The temporary portal is in a ravine outside of town and the others will have secured the area. Can you give me a hand with these crates?"

"Why are you keeping your cloaking device on now that I know what's there?" the lieutenant asked, as I helped Paul maneuver the invisible train of floating crates through the portal.

"The cloak hides them from the automatic security filters," Sue explained. "It's how we move things that aren't really allowed. It's been a pleasure knowing you, Lieutenant, and I hope we meet again someday."

"Drop in any time," he said, gesturing at the portal. "I don't suppose I have to worry about an alien invasion?"

"My team and I are the only ones who can operate the portal," I told him. "Well, my mentor, and the engineers, of course, but they don't count."

Spot took his favorite blanket in his mouth, shook his head back and forth to get it settled over his back, and then trotted through the portal without a backward glance. We manhandled Helen's oversized roll-aways through the narrow office space, and then she walked through the portal as well, followed by Sue with her cats. Or maybe they were our cats now. I'm still confused.

"Good luck," the lieutenant said, offering me a firm handshake.

"You too. Listen, there are going to be plenty of alien tourists showing up on this world, but you'll get an influx of shady types too, some of them selling shares in asteroid mining operations and the like. Don't believe any of it."

"Thanks. I'll let you lock the door," he said. "I presume this thing will shut itself down after you go through?"

"I'll close it from the other side." I shut the door after the lieutenant and threw the deadbolt, even though there was nobody left on the planet who could access the portal other than myself. My phone vibrated in my pocket. I knew I had forgotten something.

"If It Breaks. Mark speaking," I answered reflexively.

"Just calling to say goodbye," Pffift said. "My crew have been working overtime growing body parts in the vats and I should be able to pass as human within a few days. Any words of wisdom you'd care to pass along?"

"Technically, I shouldn't be helping you at all, but I guess I can share an edited version of my memories from the last month or so to give you an idea of how things really work here." I remotely hacked into the high-speed network of the Hanker's lander just to show that I could and shot him the download. "Pffift? I'm trusting you to keep this confidential. Alright?"

Postscript

The Regent of Eniniac licked her crystal ball clean at the appointed time and stared into the haze. Her magic pierced the vast distances of the void, and a familiar face slowly came into focus.

"Hello, Dearest," she spoke through her mind.

"My one and only love," came the reply. "Once again your wisdom has proved superior to my own. I never realized how much I needed a vacation until you forced me to take one."

"Are you eating well?"

"Like a king," the Archmage replied. "All of my needs are catered to as well as if I were staying at a luxury resort."

"I received a surprise visit from the Library representative on the League's executive council seeking our support for an upcoming vote. He mentioned running into you on some backwater planet and said he'd never seen you looking so relaxed."

"I was meaning to ask you to pick out a nice gift to express my thanks to him for not blowing my cover. Maybe one of those decorative wooden bowls the Ferrymen are selling—even AI must need a place to put little things. Is it possible to purchase such goods on Eniniac?"

"They opened a reservation-direct outlet store here over a thousand years ago," the regent replied patiently. Her husband had never been good with practical matters, and as much as she missed him, it was easier running a planet of mages without his well-meaning interference. "I buy hand-woven baskets from the Ferrymen to give out as baby gifts to our staff, and the outlet sells lovely retirement rugs as well."

"Oh. Listen, my love. The inhabitants at my last stop developed a form of distributed cryptocurrency with no magical protection. It's widely used for criminal activities and is completely anonymous, so I raided the wallets of all the cybercriminals and invested the proceeds in jaw exercisers that the natives use for a strange game with racquets. I prefer the used ones myself. The new ones have a strange odor and too much fur on them."

"Do I need to dispatch a ship to pick up a cargo?"

"No. The natives are utterly reliant on their world-wide network for business, even though it's entirely unsecure. I was able to arrange for collection and warehousing, and I contracted directly with a Hanker exploration vessel to deliver the shipment as soon as they reach capacity."

"That's nice, dear. As I've gotten older I've found that gnawing bones hurts my teeth."

"And that's not all. I've had an idea for an invention that could reduce our scribal costs by fifty percent..."

Spot went on to describe the process of manufacturing carbon paper using hard wax and powdered ink to get around the technology ban that would prevent the use of the polymer-based coatings currently employed on Earth. He decided to save the miracle of the ballpoint pen for a future treat.

About the Author

E. M. Foner lives in Northampton, MA with an imaginary German Shepherd who's been trained to bite bankers. The author welcomes reader comments at e_foner@yahoo.com.

Other books by the author:

Meghan's Dragon

Turing Test

Date Night on Union Station

Alien Night on Union Station

High Priest on Union Station

Spy Night on Union Station

Carnival on Union Station

Wanderers on Union Station

Vacation on Union Station

Guest Night on Union Station

Word Night on Union Station

Party Night on Union Station

Review Night on Union Station

Family Night on Union Station

Book Night on Union Station

LARP Night on Union Station

Career Night on Union Station

84367403R00153

Made in the USA
San Bernardino, CA
07 August 2018